FORSAKEN

THE FALLEN SIREN SERIES

S. J. HARPER

FORSAKEN: THE FALLEN SIREN SERIES
Published worldwide by All Romance eBooks, LLC
Safety Harbor, FL 34695
AllRomanceeBooks.com

PUBLISHER'S NOTE
This is a work of fiction and any resemblance to persons, living
or dead, or business establishments, events, or locales is
coincidental.

ISBN: 978-1-943576-17-3

First Printing, July 2015

PRAISE FOR THE FALLEN SIREN SERIES

"One entertaining and fast-paced read. Best of all? Zack, the wildly sexy werewolf FBI agent! What better crime-fighting partner could a girl have?"

—Jennifer Ashley, *New York Times* bestselling author of *Tiger Magic*

"*Cursed* is the perfect blend of magic, mystery, and romance. Emma and Zack are strong, noble characters who are trying to overcome their dark pasts, and their quests for redemption will make your heart hurt. This is a series you need to read now."

—Sandy Williams, author of the *Shadow Reader* series

"A promising new writing collaboration. . . . After delivering a hefty helping of danger and drama, Harper then sets the groundwork for more fast-paced adventures."

—*RT Book Reviews* (4 stars)

"Authors Samantha Sommersby and Jeanne C. Stein (the writing team that is S. J. Harper) have created something wonderful with the Fallen Siren series."

—Wit and Sin

"I love the story, I love the world, I love the concept, and I love the characters."

—Fangs for the Fantasy

"A good mix of traditional mythology and contemporary UF."

—Scorching Book Reviews

ALSO BY S. J. HARPER

Captured
Cursed
Reckoning
Forsaken

DEDICATION

To the readers who stepped into our world and welcomed Emma and Zack into your hearts. We thank you.

ACKNOWLEDGMENTS

We want to give special recognition to Aaron, Angie, Mario, Warren and Jeff of the Pearl Street Critique Group. Phil, Jeannette and Steve for being good to Jeanne and one another. Bill, Beverly, and Max for being there day in and day out for Sam. The S.J. Harper street team for believing in us from the get-go and their tireless enthusiasm. Editor Jessica Wade and the Penguin team for their early support of the series. Editor David Kane for his expertise. The media relations department of the San Diego Police Department, New York Police Department, and the FBI's office of public affairs for answering all of our questions. Any mistakes within this work are our own.

Siren

noun

1. One of three sisters ejected from Mount Olympus by Zeus and cursed by Demeter for failing to prevent Hades from kidnapping Persephone.

2. An immortal goddess bound to earth who, in search of her own salvation, saves others from peril.

3. A beautiful and powerful seductress, capable of infiltrating the minds of others in order to extract truth or exert influence.

FORSAKEN

THE FALLEN SIREN SERIES

S. J. HARPER

CHAPTER ONE

Sunday, September 8
Robby Maitlan has been missing for 34 hours.

I've learned that it can take a lifetime to mend a broken heart. Right here, right now, I'm ready to stop suffering this one. To stop suffering altogether. I glance over at Zack who is sound asleep. He didn't get any rest Friday night, thanks to Demeter. He was too preoccupied with feeling betrayed, manipulated, played the fool. Just as Demeter intended. Fuck Demeter. Fuck the world. I'm not giving up. I'm not giving in. I have a role to play, a duty to perform, a failure to make up for. It's what I do, who I am.

A Siren is a Siren. A sexual creature, born of Gaia. I'm one of three, cursed by Demeter thousands of years ago for failing to protect Persephone. It's for this I atone, for this I pay. It's the reason I work for the FBI and search for the missing. It's the reason I avoid love at all costs. Finding the missing brings me closer to redemption.

Finding love? I swallow hard. That always ends in ruin and death. Once again, my gaze drifts to my partner, Zack, a dark, rugged werewolf who was formerly, and quite secretly, a badass black ops assassin. Also, formerly, my lover. We met during a case in Charleston about a year and a half ago. The attraction was instant, giving into it seemingly safe. The assignment was to be temporary after all. He was to go his way. I was to go mine. There was to be no contact between us. And there wasn't until he transferred to San Diego, to my unit. Until he became my partner both in and out of bed. Until we fell in love and I made the only choice I could. I took his memories to save his life.

"Can I get you anything else?" the flight attendant asks quietly.

I hand her my empty cup and shake my head.

She moves on down the aisle.

I transfer the case file I've been perusing onto the seat between Zack and me along with my laptop and cell phone. I've read the dossier on real estate mogul and philanthropist Roger Maitlan a half-dozen times along with what little is known about the kidnapping of his seven-year-old son, Robby. Maitlan's missing child is the reason we're on our way to the Big Apple. The reason our boss, Jimmy Johnson, denied the request Zack made for transfer just yesterday morning.

I notice the light above the forward lavatory has turned from red to green. I consider waking Zack for a fraction of a second before deciding against. I'm agile, limber, and frankly not looking forward to once again facing his ire. I quietly unbuckle, lift up the arm separating the window and middle seats, then slide over. I stand in so much as I can, considering the outcropping of overhead bins, and turn to face him. Left hand on the middle seat, I lift my right leg up and over his. He doesn't flinch. There's no alteration in his breathing. My toe touches the ground, and I begin to shift my weight to the foot that's now firmly planted in the aisle. His hand brushes my thigh, his eyes open.

He sits up straighter in his chair. "You could have woken me and asked me to move." His tone is irritable, bordering on accusing.

I avoid eye contact, avoid his touch. "Let's pretend I did," I say before slipping out of the row and making my way toward the front of the plane. I feel his eyes on me. Never did I imagine viewing an airplane lavatory as a refuge. I take care of the most immediate needs first, then I wash my hands. When I reach for the paper towels, I catch a glimpse of myself in the mirror. I have to admit, I look a little worse for wear. Considering what I've been through in the past twenty-four hours, that shouldn't come as a surprise.

This time yesterday Zack and I were staging the rescue of ten missing girls, all young, blonde virgins—pawns in a power play between two ruling vampire factions. The losing side led by the now dead Southern vampire King, Philippe Lamont. The winner? Kallistos Kouros. My betrayer, my savior, and now the Sovereign of both the West and the South. Kallistos and I had been sharing a bed for the better part of six months. The no-strings-attached relationship worked for us both—the vampire who made no demands, except for the most exquisite sexual ones, and the Siren who could fulfill those demands without sacrificing her heart. Only in the end my heart did suffer as I watched him take the lives of humans to ensure his position, grow his kingdom, and increase his power. I'd like to condemn him, but I can't. Kallistos told me what to expect of him more times than I could count. And I have to admit he's delivered supremely on both his promise to be there when needed and to disappoint. If he hadn't healed me two nights ago, I'd be gone. Not dead, Demeter would never have allowed that, forced to move on to another life. Problem is, I'm not done with this one.

I lean closer to the mirror and study my appearance, seeking assurance that the two spells I pay my best friend Liz for are still firmly in place. The first, a reverse glamour that hides my true appearance and furnishes me with the wholesome, plain-Jane facade I've become so accustomed to seeing. The second, a dampening spell that diminishes both my innate powers of seduction and the nifty little side effect that makes me the most reliable lie detector ever. I realize that Liz, who is not only the baddest witch this side of the Mississippi, but my touchstone when it comes to matters of the heart, doesn't know what happened in the last couple days between Kallistos and me, between Zack and me, between Demeter and me— that I'm on my way to New York, that everything is different, my life changed.

I make a half-hearted effort to smooth down my hair, which is long, dark, and pulled back into a simple ponytail. I can't help noticing that my skin, normally fair and unblemished, is paler than usual.

Not because of a lack of makeup. I never wear makeup. No mascara. No lip-gloss. Nothing. I reach up and pinch my cheeks. It doesn't help. The inside of my lower eyelid contains only the barest hint of pink. I'm anemic. I've lost too much blood. Not during the mission. Though there was plenty of blood shed last night, none of it was mine. My near death experience came this morning at the hand of my favorite vindictive goddess, Demeter. After she betrayed me. After Zack discovered my betrayal of him.

Zack.

The only innocent in this mess.

I may not want to face his wrath, have to endure his judgment, but I deserve it. I've wronged him and I can't make it right, not if I want him to live. I stiffen my spine before sliding open the latch to the door. By the time I make my way down the aisle to our row, Zack is standing. The hard expression he's been wearing all morning has softened. He has my cell phone in his grasp. As I slide into my chair he hands it to me.

"You forgot to switch your cell to airplane mode. A message came in from Kallistos."

Zack normally refers to the vampire King as His Royal Undead or Tall, Dark, and Pasty. The mere fact that he's using his name means whatever's in the message is serious.

While I excel at giving orders, I'm terrible at following them. Despite what you may think, I care, deeply. Your wounds were severe, your continued pain palpable. To fully heal you might need more blood, not to mention a friend. I'm offering, but don't expect you will accept. I'm calling in the cavalry. Expect to hear from Liz. ~ K

My eyes burn. I set the phone down on the seat between Zack and me, then once again pick up and open the file. The words on the page are a blur. Our connection out of Chicago was cancelled last night due to a storm, and I didn't get much sleep. Zack reaches over and takes it from me.

"Did he hurt you? Did he punish you because we…" The words are spoken softly, with a tenderness that makes the ache I'm feeling even worse.

Because we made love?

I shake my head. "It wasn't Kallistos."

He waits a beat and swallows hard before asking the next question. This time his voice is even lower. "When you passed out, I thought… Did *I* hurt you?"

"No." A moment passes. I meet his gaze, force what I know is a shaky smile. "Yes." I turn to look out the window. "But not in the way you mean. And I will get over it. So will you."

He leans in close, the anger has returned. "I want my memories back."

After we saved the girls, Demeter granted me a reprieve. Only it wasn't a reprieve, not really. It was a set up, a web spun by the most calculating spider of them all, and I fell right into it. Giving myself to Zack, opening up fully, letting him see the real me. Believing it could last when it couldn't. Not when my Siren scent was destined to link back to evidence Zack had that we'd been lovers before and that magic had been used on him to erase those memories.

I watch the clouds pass by. My voice sounds as

distant as the land far below. "That won't change anything."

"It would restore a measure of trust between us."

How I wish that were true. I remind myself why I avoided the truth and used the spell to begin with. Zack would never be satisfied with the kind of relationship Kallistos and I had. He deserves more. He would want more and he'd fight for it. He'd fight against a Goddess. He'd fight, he'd lose, and he'd die.

It's happened before.

I say what's true, "It would only leave you with more questions."

"Questions you won't answer."

"Can't answer," I counter.

"Bullshit. You know, if your goal is to keep me pissed off, I'd say your work here is done."

"It's *not* done. You *can* trust me."

"Trust you to do what?"

"To keep you safe," the words are flung at him in a hiss. I quickly add, "To do my job."

"To keep me safe." Zack grows still, quiet. For a long while, he says nothing. Then, "Kallistos didn't punish you, but someone did." He sighs. Shakes his head. "I suppose it doesn't matter. Whatever rules were broken, whatever dangers or threats remain. The mess that's been made is as much my fault as yours. Maybe more my fault. I was foolish enough to believe that I'd found a *partner.* That maybe, just maybe, I could escape the past, have a future."

For as long as I've known him, Zack has always said the word partner like it really means something.

For the first time, I realize how much significance the word really holds for him, how much he's wanted a partner in work, in bed, in love, in life. I let my head fall back against the headrest. I'm emotionally and physically exhausted. "Take it from me, the past is inescapable. The future a place of infinite unknowns."

"What does that leave us with, Emma?" Zack asks.

"What does that leave us with?" I repeat, letting the question roll around in my head even though I already know the answer. I nod at the folder he's holding in his hand. "That. The job. You and I, together, will find that boy." I say it with conviction then add, "Until we do, the rest gets pushed aside."

Zack opens the file and picks up the five by seven photo of a smiling Robby Maitlan in a baseball uniform. "Until we find him," he agrees. "Eye on the ball."

"Eye on the ball," I repeat, grateful to be back on solid ground. Grateful to be doing what I do best: finding the missing.

Zack hands me the photo. "The kid looks just like his dad."

Just a few weeks ago Roger Maitlan's photo was on the cover of some magazine at the grocery store's checkout.

"Sure does," I agree, silently repeating the same words I do every time I get a new case. *Redemption could be one rescue away.*

I try to hand the photo back. Zack doesn't notice. He seems to be preoccupied with a note in the file telling us we're to be met at the airport in

New York by an agent from one of the FBI's Child Abduction Rapid Deployment Teams. When Zack and I first met, he was assigned to one of the CARD teams himself.

"You know her?" I ask.

He shakes his head. "I know of her," he replies. "I was assigned to the Southeast team. She's in the Northeast division. We never actually worked a case together but we've gone to some of the same training classes, attended some of the same debriefings."

The announcement overhead tells us to put our tray tables up and return our seatbacks to an upright position. I hear the landing gear come down. The ground below is getting closer. Though I know the opposite is true, the further we descend, the faster we seem to be moving. I grow quiet, contemplative.

"You miss it," Zack says.

"What?"

"Flying."

He's right. It doesn't matter that it's been scores of centuries since Demeter stripped me of my wings, leaving only a tattoo in their place. I miss the sensation as much today as I did the day I lost the ability to soar on my own. I close my eyes, absorb the rush of the speed, imagine the feel of the wind, and brace for landing.

CHAPTER TWO

We're gathering our things together to deplane. "So you'll know her by sight?"

"Oh, yeah."

The way he says it makes me curious, but the line is moving and I don't have time to follow up. When we exit the gangway, Zack is immediately swallowed up by the crowd at the gate. Fortunately, his height provides me with an advantage and I'm able to follow past the cramped rows of chairs, kiosks filled with quick meals to go, and hundreds of weary travelers. Welcome to La Guardia. Finally, we spill out into the baggage area. Since we both carried on there's nothing there for us to collect, only our ride. It takes Zack just a second or two to spot her.

I can see why he'd remembered Regina Torres. She is a striking woman. Tall, dark hair worn loose around her shoulders, beautiful green eyes, light brown skin. Her face is more angular than classic oval, with high cheekbones, a straight nose and a no-nonsense cut to her jaw. Her make-up isn't exactly subtle, but her overall look remains professional. She's wearing black slacks and a grey cable-knit, form-fitting sweater. A blazer completes the outfit, expertly tailored to conceal the weapon she no doubt has holstered on her hip or at the small of her back. Agent Torres may have been sent to welcome us, but the expression she throws our way upon spying Zack makes me feel anything but.

She slides the cell phone she's had in her hand into the pocket of her coat. "I have a car waiting outside." No smile. No handshake offered. She merely turns on her heels and strides toward the exit. "Follow me."

"Is Torres always this warm and fuzzy?" I whisper to Zack.

I get the famous Armstrong shrug and with it the impression that Zack's not quite so surprised by her reaction.

"Let's not keep her waiting," he says.

We hurry to catch up and find her outside standing by a standard issue black Suburban parked in a "police vehicles only" space. She opens the rear passenger door, as if expecting Zack and me to climb in the back. Instead, Zack motions me in and takes the front passenger seat. There is a decided ratcheting up of coldness when she slams the door shut behind him.

As soon as she climbs into the SUV Zack tries to make nice. "Thanks for meeting us. I don't believe we've ever officially been introduced. Zack Armstrong. This is my partner, Emma Monroe."

Left with no choice, she takes his offered hand for the briefest of moments. "I know who you are." The statement is punctuated by the sound of her seatbelt clicking securely into place.

I lean forward, inserting myself between them. "Normally Zack and I have to actually spend some time in a jurisdiction before pissing off the locals in charge. I've had a rough couple of days. So, between us, I'd rather you just come out with the reason for this warm welcome. I don't have the energy to guess."

We're on the road now, but that doesn't stop Torres from glancing accusingly at Zack. "*You* probably don't have to guess, do you?"

"You were assigned lead on this case," Zack says, "and you resent our presence. Maitlin's request."

"Is that what you call it?" Torres snaps back. "A request? More like a demand. He insisted that I call you in. No explanation why. And not as a liaison or consultant. No. He expects you to run the show. And son of a bitch if my boss didn't fold." She takes her eyes off the road to look at Zack. "Want to explain why? Because this makes no sense to me."

I'm waiting with bated breath. I'd like to know the answer to that, too. Zack gave me no indication while we were on the plane that we'd be walking into a political nightmare. But from where I'm sitting, he had to have known. I assumed it was Johnson and Torres' boss that decided we should be involved. Now it seems clear it was Maitlan, the father of the kidnapped kid, that requested Zack, and that it was the powers that be who acquiesced. Pretty un-fucking-heard-of. I'm as interested in the answer as Torres.

But Zack's response doesn't appease either of us. "Men like Maitlan are used to getting what they want. It doesn't *have* to make sense." His tone loses its edge, "Wouldn't this time be better spent going over the details of the case? We read the file on the plane but I'd like to hear what happened from you. You must know more by now."

Torres' glare softens. From my vantage point in the back seat, I see her shoulders begin to relax. She knows Zack is right, it doesn't matter why we're here. A child is missing. That should be our focus. She begins to recite the details as if she's done it a dozen times by rote, her tone dispassionate. "Friday night, Roger Maitlan hosted his annual black-tie party for cancer research. It's a once-a-year fundraiser, very exclusive. Maitlan and his millionaire friends get together and open their wallets for a cause that is near to his heart. His wife died of brain cancer two years ago. Since then he's devoted time and resources to finding a cure. The only thing more important to him is his son."

"And while Maitlan was using his power and influence for something altruistic, mingling with New York's upper crust at MoMA, Robby was taken," Zack interjects.

"What else do we know?" I ask.

"Two masked gunman intercepted the doorman as he entered the building during a change of shift. Normally there's a doorman on duty at all times and the entry's kept securely locked. The gunmen had it all timed. I wouldn't say the job was carried out with military precision, but at least one of them had been inside before, was familiar with the procedure for shift change, the location of the cameras."

I'm thumbing through the file as Torres is

talking. There are photographs of the building and of the views from the lobby security cams before they were shot out. "So, the first thing they did was shoot out the cameras?"

"No," Torres answers shortly. "The first thing they did was subdue the doorman coming on duty. They held him at gunpoint, forced him to act like everything was normal even though his wrists were cable-tied behind his back. As soon as they gained entrance, one of the gunmen swept his feet right out from under him. Duct tape was used to bind his legs and cover his mouth. He landed hard, got knocked out. Has a pretty bad concussion. They haven't discharged him yet. He doesn't remember much."

Zack nods. "The second doorman sustained some injuries as well?"

"A few cracked ribs and a broken nose while in the lobby. He's a month shy of retirement, but he went down fighting. According to the surveillance video, he got a punch or two in before the cameras were shot out. Once upstairs, he was cold-cocked but good. When he came to, his hands were cable-tied behind his back, the babysitter dead, and Robby gone."

"You've questioned him?"

"Yeah, but he was in a lot of pain and still pretty shaken up. The babysitter was just a kid, seventeen. She lived in the building and he'd watched her grow up."

"Any sign that Robby might have been injured?" Zack asks.

"No. There was no evidence of a struggle. Then again, the boy is just over fifty pounds. He could have been easily subdued. The only thing we know for sure is that the kidnappers exited through the parking garage with a large duffle, one big enough for a seven-year-old to fit in. The footage showed only their backs, but it's clearly them."

"Why shoot out the cameras in the lobby but not the garage?" I ask.

Torres frowns. "We don't know. Maybe they didn't know about the surveillance in the garage. The building manager reported those cameras were just recently installed."

"One dead, two injured," says Zack. "Not your normal stealthy kidnapping. These guys wanted to send a message."

We're winding through the streets of Manhattan. Despite the traffic, Torres doesn't miss a beat. "What's the message?"

"They're ruthless," I mutter, still looking at the photographs. "Forensics find anything?"

Torres shakes her head. "Nothing yet. They were in and out quickly. Wore gloves. Likely used silencers. No one reported hearing anything when the girl was shot."

"Do we have a description of the getaway car?"

"No. They walked out of the garage. We have no idea which way they went or what kind of getaway vehicle they used."

"No cameras on the street?"

"Not for a couple of blocks."

"What about ballistics?"

"The lab is working on that."

Zack has been quiet during this exchange. Now he asks, "And no ransom demand?"

"Not yet."

It's been years since I've been in New York. Some things have changed since the last century, but much has remained the same. I recognize that we're headed toward the Upper East Side—one of the most expensive and exclusive areas in Manhattan.

"How's Maitlan taking it?" Zack asks.

"Like an ego-maniac who's used to being in control."

We're paused at a light. Torres rolls down her window and shouts at a young couple who decided to stop in the middle of the crosswalk and argue with one another. Rather than move on, they interpret her attempt to chastise them as an invitation and approach.

"Can you point us in the direction of Central Park?" asks the wide-eyed damsel. The accent is Southern, her clothing more appropriate for a church picnic than a late summer trek through the Big Apple.

"Oh for fuck's sake," mutters Torres, flashing her badge. "Do I look like a tour guide to you?"

Zack, ever the gentleman leans forward. "Morning! Where ya'll from?"

"Goose Creek, South Carolina," the man pipes in. "It's—"

"North of Charleston," interjects Zack. "I was born and raised in South Cacalacky." Despite the chorus of horns around us and the steam coming out of Torres' ears, he quickly points them in the direction of Central Park.

Welcome to New York. I watch the young couple walk away as Torres guns the engine, pitching me forward. Some things never do change.

Five minutes and two turns later, we come up on an imposing building on East 65th Street. Looking skyward, the building rises thirty or more stories. If I haven't gotten turned around myself, the west facing windows should have a sweeping view of Central Park, which is now less than half a block away. We slow to a snail's pace. A large contingent of television vans, representing both local and national networks, line the sidewalks in front.

I take quick inventory. Several crews are actively filming. Uniformed police stand guard at the door. A narrow alley off to the side of the building is blocked off with crime scene tape and a blockade. "The vultures have descended. Can we get past them?"

"A homicide and kidnapping in this neighborhood is a hard story to keep quiet," Torres says. "The minute the call came across the police scanners, the circus was inevitable. We've done our best to keep the details of the kidnapping and our involvement to a minimum, but as you can see—"

"It's going to be damn near impossible with this level of scrutiny," Zack finishes.

Torres steers past the reporters and cameramen milling around the building's entrance then turns into the alley. The blockade is removed allowing her to pull into the parking garage. She pauses long enough at the iron gate to punch in a key code. It lifts and we pull forward. A security guard emerges from a second gate, which appears to be a newly constructed booth.

"Agent Torres," he nods.

She gestures in our general direction as she introduces us. "This is Agent Armstrong and this is Agent Monroe."

"I'm going to have to see some identification." The request is made without a hint of apology.

After he examines our credentials, the second gate is raised.

"This one looks new," I observe.

"The installation was finished just hours ago," Torres says as we pull into a nearby space. "Maitlan paid for it himself. Had a crew working all night to get it set up. Case of closing the barn door after the horse has already escaped, if you ask me. But he owns the majority interest in the building and can do as he damn well pleases." She shoots Zack a pointed look. "And we know what Maitlan wants, Maitlan gets." The statement is punctuated with a plastic smile.

Zack's expression remains neutral and he says nothing, but I see signs that his exasperation with Torres' attitude is growing. He slams the car door shut a little too sharply upon exiting. He doesn't wait for her to lead the way to the elevator.

"We're heading to the one in the middle," Torres calls out.

I quicken my pace to catch up with Zack and take a second to whisper, "Is this going to be a problem?"

There's a telltale tick in his jaw, his fist clenches. "We'll smooth it out somehow."

Torres joins us and punches numbers into yet another keypad. The doors slide open. She steps in first, barely waiting for Zack and me to follow.

Inside there's only one button. She presses it and we're instantly whooshed upwards.

I lean against the back wall. The space is larger than my dining room. Torres and Zack have managed to take full advantage and stand on opposite sides. Torres stares straight ahead, her features set in stone. Zack's posture is rigid, feet hip-width apart, hands clasped behind his back in a classic parade rest.

"I'd like to interview the doorman again, the one they took up to the apartment," he says.

"Deke Jackson? We taped the interview. I can show—"

He doesn't even let her finish. "Get him in here. I want to talk to him myself."

So much for smoothing it out.

When the doors open, any hope I have to take the tension down a notch is dashed. Crime scene tape still in place to the left of the elevator, where I presume the babysitter was killed, and around the front door, where the second doorman was left unconscious. Dark red bloodstains paint a grisly, Technicolor picture. I recall the photo of the girl, her body splayed out at odd angles, lying face down. A chill washes over me. Not because it's the worst I've seen, but because I know without a doubt that anyone vicious enough to kill one innocent child in cold blood would not hesitate to kill a second.

I look up at Zack. He's already taken in the scene. Now he's watching me. His face reflects the same concern.

"Zack! Thank God you're here."

It's Maitlan. I recognize him from the photos in

the file Johnson gave us, not to mention the ones plastered all over the press. Maitlan's polished PR team maintains careful control over his image. The forty-year-old with piercing blue eyes and dark hair graying at the temples is almost always presented in a dark suit, classic white shirt and tie. The photos of the mogul and his family lining the hallway, some adorned with remnants of blood splatter, belie that singular impression. Maitlan may appear the consummate icon of capitalist success in the press, but the pictures on the wall tell another story. They show a Roger Maitlan with laughing eyes and a warm smile—a loving father in private moments. In the first, Robby appears to be about five. He's riding atop Maitlan's shoulders, dressed in a baseball uniform, trophy in hand. In the second, Maitlan and his son are cheek-to-cheek, leaning in to blow out three candles on what appears to be a homemade cake. Then there's a third, taken in what could be Central Park. Maitlan is standing alongside a woman, a natural beauty with short cropped flaming red hair and an easy smile. He's tossing his son high into the air, his strong arms are outstretched, poised to catch him.

"That one was taken when Corrine was in remission the first time," he says, tears in his eyes. This Maitlan's face is pale and drawn, the lines around his mouth are tight with anxiety and fear. His shoulders bunch under the tuxedo jacket he's still wearing from last night.

Maitlan reaches for Zack's hand and gives it a friendly shake, "I appreciate you coming, Zack. My office is this way, we can talk in private."

Okay, it's obvious that there's something Zack hadn't bothered to mention. He and Roger Maitlan know each other. But there's no opportunity to demand an explanation. Maitlan leads Zack down the hallway to a set of stairs, a second entryway. This one is more formal than the one upstairs. It's lined with statues, the walls with paintings, and tiled with expensive marble. I follow, as does Torres. Maitlan reaches a doorway at the end of the hall, opens the door and quickly ushers Zack in. Then, without so much as a glance back, the door snaps shut behind them.

For the first time, I sympathize with Torres. We look at each other. I imagine our expressions are mirror images of exasperation and indignation.

"And here I was, taking all of this personally," she mutters. "Welcome to the club. I think I'll go check with forensics, see if they have anything new. Want to come?"

The sound of a door reopening draws our attention.

Zack steps out and motions toward me. "Emma, join us?"

"Sure." So much for female bonding. "Torres was just about to go get an update on forensics." I turn back to Torres, "You've already had a chance to personally interview Mr. Maitlan. How about you give us fifteen, then we'll regroup?"

She relaxes a bit, nods, then turns on her heels and leaves us.

CHAPTER THREE

Before stepping into the room, I pause in front of Zack. "After this, you and I are going to have a conversation."

Maitlan is standing behind a well-worn walnut desk gazing out of Cathedral windows at what I'm sure is a twenty-million-dollar view of Central Park. "Zack said you'd find my boy," he turns and for the first time he *really* looks at me. "He told me there's no one he'd rather work with in a situation like this." Maitlan holds out his hand.

I grasp it. Despite his current vulnerability and obvious exhaustion, Maitlan's shake is firm, confident, practiced. "Emma Monroe," I say before taking a moment to check the room.

The back wall is filled top to bottom with expansive bookcases. A wrought iron circular staircase leads up to the second level which functions as a reading loft with cozy chairs and a fireplace that's a twin to the one Zack's now standing next to.

"Let's sit," Maitlan gestures toward a set of sofas by Zack. He and Zack claim one. I take the other. On a coffee table between us there's a tray containing a crystal carafe of amber colored liquid and a matching set of old-fashioned glasses. Without preamble and despite the early hour Maitlan pours up a couple fingers and with an unceremonious clunk places a glass in front of each of us.

"Zack says you'll have questions and that if I want your help in finding my son, I better answer." Maitlan swallows his drink in one gulp. "Robby means everything to me. You have to find him."

"We'll get him back," Zack interjects, promising something he shouldn't. This is personal for him, very personal.

I leave my drink untouched. "The clock is ticking. We need the truth."

Zack waves an arm in Maitlan's direction. "Fire away," he tells me.

My first question isn't for Maitlan. I face Zack. "Explain the connection between the two of you."

Zack pauses only long enough to down what I assume to be whiskey. "Maitlan and I met in the Middle East, around the time I was trying to extricate myself from my former employers. They wanted Maitlan to take on a project in Iraq—the kind of project that would benefit them and no one else. The deal had corruption written all over it. Maitlan had a reputation for both being a patriot and being willing to bend the rules, but what these guys wanted was too risky. And had political implications that could come back and bite him in the ass."

"Not to mention it was just plain wrong. I turned the deal down," Maitlan added.

The sun, pouring in through the windows, is warm against my back. I slide off my suit jacket and roll up the sleeves of my white, cotton blouse. "I take it these men were not used to hearing the word no."

Zack's smile confirms I've made the understatement of the year. He continues, "When they saw he wasn't going to play ball, they asked me to drive him back to the airport. No harm, no foul, right?"

"Only, that's not the way the outfit works," I say.

His eyes skewer mine. "No. It isn't. And I'd been in long enough to know that. On the way to the airport, we were attacked. Seems they'd realized I wanted out and figured they'd kill two birds with one stone—get rid of Maitlan and assure my silence."

Maitlan breaks in. "Zack fought them. Kicked ass. Killed all three gunmen then managed to get us both to a safe house. I took a bullet in the shoulder. Zack got hit in the leg. At first I thought it must have nicked the femoral artery. There was so much blood." Maitlan stands and begins to pace, he's looking a little green around the gills.

Zack grins. "Sissy passed out."

"I'm still not sure how you managed to get me to that safe house."

"We laid low for a week," Zack continued, "then I got us both out of the country and back to the states."

At this Maitlan laughs. "He makes it sound so simple. In reality it was anything but." He looks at

Zack. "I owe you my life and now I'll owe you my son's."

I notice a vintage brass bar cart in the corner. It's littered with a variety of glasses, an assortment of alcohol and mixers, as well as a variety of soft drinks and bottles of water. I walk over and help myself to one. "Do you think the men who tried to kill the two of you are the same men who have your son?"

Maitlan shakes his head. "No. The evidence Zack has against them has managed to keep us both safe for this long. I don't see a reason for that changing. And it's not just Zack that I want on the case. When he transferred to San Diego I checked you out, Agent Monroe. You've made quite a reputation for yourself. I'm used to working with the best. I'm convinced if anyone can get Robby back, you two can."

I open the bottle of water and take a sip. "There's more to it than that. Torres and her team are competent, more than competent. This is about trust."

Maitlan passes a hand over his face. It's a tell that says I'm right. There *is* more to this story.

"What haven't you told Special Agent Torres? What is it you think you can't trust her with?" I ask.

"I've done some extremely stupid things since Robby's mother died." He leans forward, elbows resting on his knees and stares down into his empty glass. Color rises to his cheeks. "It's complicated."

"It always is." I reclaim my spot on the sofa across from him. "Believe me, whatever your indiscretion, I've heard it before. We're not here to judge you. We're here to find your son. Help us do that."

He nods, stands, sets his drink on the mantle of the fireplace. "I loved my wife. When she died, I was barely able to hold it together. She'd been sick for so long, you'd think I would have been prepared." His back is to us, his shoulders slump even further. "Take it from me, you're never prepared. I had a company to run. A son to raise. And there was so much scrutiny. I had to hold it together. Maintain control, so much control. Day after day until I couldn't do it anymore. After Robby went down for the night, I'd crawl into the bottle. One night his nanny crawled into bed with me. She'd lived with us since Robby was born. I trusted her."

"And that was a mistake," Zack interjected.

"Yes," Maitlan agrees. "I was drunk. We did some coke. There was a video."

The rest I can imagine. "She's been blackmailing you."

Maitlan turns to face us. "Not any longer, she's dead. I started making payments. Within a few weeks her recreational drug habit turned into a full-blown addiction. She overdosed in her apartment. There was quite a bit of cash and coke. Her property was seized."

"And with it the video?" I asked.

"I had to recover it. I confessed everything to my attorney. He put me in touch with someone who could get it back. *That* man introduced me to Elysium."

Elysium. I know it as the place where mortals who are invited by the gods spend their afterlife, those who were heroes, righteous. Something tells me this Elysium is different.

Maitlan continues, "It's a club, the kind of club that caters to every man's taste. Very private. Very exclusive."

Zack holds up his glass. "I take it we're talking about more than a place you can go to smoke cigars and drink whisky?"

That gets a small smile from the multi-billionaire. "On the surface it looks like your typical stodgy gentleman's club. Members do stop in the bar on occasion, have a drink, a bite to eat, smoke a cigar. But most, including me, go there for sex. Encounters that are uncomplicated, even anonymous if you wish it. Fantasies made to order. It's run by a woman named Eve Devlin. There's nothing she can't arrange... for a price."

"And what does all of this have to do with your son's kidnapping?" I ask, my patience wearing thin.

"I believe Eve has Robby."

My partner asks the question that's on both of our minds. "And why would Eve Devlin take your son?"

Maitlan waits a beat before replying. "Because I took from her the only thing she loved more than Elysium. I'm responsible for the death of her daughter."

Zack and I exchange looks.

"She was your nanny? The one that overdosed?" I ask.

"No. Eve's daughter, Amanda, was employed at Elysium. She wasn't one of the working girls. She managed the schedule, kept the books. Nice, though rather plain. Despite her upbringing she was shy and somewhat sheltered. There was a social awkwardness about her. I don't believe we'd ever had a conversation that didn't involve me booking a reservation until that night."

I interrupt him then. "I'm not a therapist, Mr. Maitlan. And Zack sure as hell isn't a priest. If you're going to confess—

"I didn't murder Amanda, if that's what your thinking."

"Just tell us what happened," prompts Zack.

"It was just a couple weeks ago. I'd called in and requested—" He falters, clears his throat, "A favorite of mine. Amanda took the reservation as usual and assured me the girl would be available when I arrived. Only when I showed up, it was Amanda waiting for me in the room. Naked. In bed."

He pauses, shuts his eyes for a moment as though dredging up the memory is painful. When he continues, his voice is once again calm, controlled. "I'd stopped in the bar, had a few drinks before going upstairs. At first I thought I had the wrong room. I apologized and started to back out. That's when Amanda professed her love for me. I thought she was joking. And I did the worst thing I could have done. I laughed. She unraveled before my eyes. It became clear she'd concocted a fantasy in which we were a couple. She kept saying that night was to be the beginning for us. She would be a mother for Robby. A wife to me. I would never have to frequent her mother's place again."

He pauses again, a look of conflicted anger and

sadness darkening his eyes. "She was fragile, and only a girl, barely twenty. The more I tried to calm her, the more hysterical she became. For obvious reasons, the rooms are soundproof. No one was going to come to the rescue. I left her there and went in search of help."

"What happened next?" I ask.

Maitlan shakes his head. "I don't know exactly. In an effort to maintain discretion, I went in search of Eve. I'd barely gotten the words out when she muttered 'not again' and ordered me out, banning me from ever coming back. A few days later I learned Amanda committed suicide. Broke the mirror in the adjoining bathroom and slit her wrists. Eve might have saved her life if she'd immediately called 911. But there was Elysium and its clients to protect."

"So she hesitated. She let her daughter die and instead of accepting responsibility for that choice..."

"She blames me. The day of Amanda's funeral I received an enormous spray of orange lilies. I looked it up. They symbolize hatred. The card simply read: *An eye for an eye*. One week to the day, Robby was taken. She sent the flowers. She took my son. I don't have proof, but I know it."

"Why not call in an anonymous tip, have vice go in and search the place?" I ask.

"Because they can't be trusted. Eve doesn't just service the wealthy, she also allows in select government officials, upper echelon law enforcement, celebrities, and powerful criminals. She has leverage. A call to the police to report the goings on at Elysium would likely result in...

nothing. Plus, Robby won't be there. Eve's far too smart for that. I'm going to get my son back and I'm going to need my own leverage. *That's* why you're here."

Zack's gaze moves from me to Maitlan. "Speak plainly, Roger, tell us what you want." His tone says he already knows. I lean forward.

Maitlan's entire body relaxes from the weight of relief. "Eve keeps a ledger. Not on a computer, I'm talking about an actual paper journal. Details about who her customers are, their *preferences,* how much they've paid over the years." He's speaking to Zack, not me. "I want you to steal it. I know how you protected yourself from your former employers. It's worked. It's kept us both safe. I know you're capable of breaking into Eve's office and getting that book. And, I know I can trust you to do it. I'll pay you anything. We'd have the leverage I need, then we could arrange a swap."

"The book for your son," Zack says.

"Eve will have no choice." Maitlan slumps against his chair. "Eve plans to kill Robby. That's what the message on the card meant. I know it. But if we can get our hands on that book, she'll have no choice but to return him. To protect herself not only from the police, but from her clients. As I see it, it's the only way."

I look over at Zack. His eyes are on me. Trying to gauge my reaction. I'm trying to gauge his. Is he really considering this? Before I can ask he turns to face Maitlan.

"You're right that I leveraged my freedom with information that could hurt not only my employers, but the governments of several countries as well. It's working...for now. But it's a standoff. A dangerous one. Not a perfect solution."

"It's a crazy idea," I pipe up. "Someone has to be the voice of reason here. First of all, you're assuming a lot. We don't know it's Eve behind the kidnapping. Even if she is, and Zack got the book, why would Eve trust that you hadn't made copies? What if you're wrong that the business is more important than the death of her daughter? Not to mention we'd be compromising the investigation and wasting precious time that we could be using to find Robby."

Zack rises. "I do think this Eve Devlin is a lead worth following."

I glare at him. "Tell me you aren't really considering—"

Before I can finish my thought, the door flies open. Torres steps into the room, a headset in her hand. "You've got a call coming in," she says to Maitlan. "No caller ID. It may be a ransom demand."

Maitlan jumps to his feet and rushes after Torres. "If it is and I can keep him on the phone long enough, you can trace it. Right?"

Zack and I follow close behind.

"If they're calling from a landline or a registered mobile, yes. We'll have the location within seconds. The phone company's been alerted," says Torres.

We cross the hallway and head into the room next door. This turns out to be a conference room with a long table down the middle. Two agents have set up their equipment here; one looks up as we enter.

He snaps his fingers at Maitlan. "Pick up line one. If it's him, keep him talking as long as possible. The longer he talks, the more information we'll have to study. And ask to speak with Robby. Be cooperative but insistent."

Maitlan grabs for the phone. With a shaking hand, he puts the receiver to his ear. "Maitlan here."

For a moment, only the ticking of the wall clock breaks the uneasy silence in the room. Torres has the headset to her ear and she's taken a seat at the table, a pad in front of her. She starts to write. Finally, Maitlan speaks.

"It might take a little more time than that, but I can get you the money," he says. Then, "Okay. I understand. Yes. I'll do exactly as you say. But I want to speak to Robby."

Once more there's silence as Maitlan listens, his face contorted in apprehension. "No. I want to speak to my son. I need to be certain he's okay. Please, you can't... No, don't hang up!"

For a terrible moment, he stares at the phone. He looks over at Torres. "He wouldn't let me talk to Robby. What if he's dead?"

"He's not," she replies calmly. "More often then not those who pay the ransom get their kids back."

The agent at the table who was monitoring the call looks up. "The call couldn't be traced. They used a burner."

"It's probably already in a dumpster somewhere," I say. "These guys know what they're doing."

Maitlan is pacing. "Why wouldn't they let me talk to him?"

"Don't read anything into it," says Zack, his voice calm. "Right now, we need to play the hand we've been dealt."

I know Zack probably heard both sides of the conversation. His werewolf hearing is exceptional, but for now, I look to Torres. "How long before the drop?"

She's torn the top page from the pad. For once, there's no hostility in her manner when she answers. "Mr. Maitlan has two hours. He needs to get the money, then walk to the Central Park Boathouse and await further instructions by the large tree outside the Express Cafe." She glances at her watch. "It's noon now. He is to be at the Boathouse with the ransom in a backpack by two. That doesn't give us much time."

"It's all the time I need." Maitlan says, heading for the door.

Zack moves to intercept him. "Slow down for just a minute."

Maitlan pushes him aside. "They said no cops." His voice is shaky. "They're watching. If they see you, suspect you're there, Robby is dead."

If he isn't already. The words go unsaid, but it's what I'm thinking, what all of us are thinking. The kidnappers have already demonstrated they have no problem with killing. Why not provide proof of life? Either they can't, or they want to keep Maitlan guessing, suffering.

"I called the president of the bank at home hours ago. We've been friends for years. He's been moving cash into the central branch all morning. I can make it to the bank and back in an hour."

"How are you going to get out without the press seeing you?" I ask. "Reporters are all over. They'll be watching the parking garage, too. There's no way for you to leave the building unnoticed."

That makes him pause. But just for an instant. "I won't leave this building. I also own majority interest in the adjoining one. When Corrine fell ill, I broke through the wall and built out the office space so I could easily work from home. It's actually in the building next door. I can access the thirty-second floor hallway from the upper level of my office. If I change into running clothes, wear a couple sweaters and the backpack under a hoodie to give me more padding—"

"It could work," interrupts Torres.

That's all Maitlan needs. "I'll change," he says, then he's out the door.

I spy a large urn on a credenza. Nearby are mugs, sugar and creamer. I tilt my head toward it. "Don't know about you, but I could use a cup of coffee."

"No thanks," replies Zack. He turns to stare out the window.

"I reached out to Deke Jackson. I had to leave a message," Torres says. When that gets no response she adds, "Do you want me to send a car and have him brought in or will my prior interview be satisfactory?"

The tension in the room is so thick, I can barely breathe. I pour myself a cup of the dark roast, take a sip of the bitter brew.

Finally, Zack shakes his head. "There's no time for me to question Mr. Jackson now." He turns to the other agents in the room. "I imagine things are going to be moving pretty fast for the next few hours. I'm going to need everyone's full cooperation."

"You've got it." The man across the table from Zack rises and offers his hand. "Riley O'Neill." My guess is that he's in his late twenties—maybe thirty. He has "new agent" written all over him—from the crisp white shirt and tasteful dark blue tie to the suit coat hung carefully over the back of his chair. I'd even bet he has oxblood wingtips under those well-creased suit pants.

Zack looks pointedly at the gentleman to O'Neill's right, the one who instructed Maitlan on how to handle the call. He's older, early fifties. His hair is close-cropped. His skin is weathered. His accent is all Brooklyn.

"Ben Bradley. Just tell us what you need." He raises his hands in a surrender posture before tilting his head toward Riley. "We're a good team. Been together for a while now, and this isn't our first rodeo. Though I can see how you might get that impression considering the baby face on Ri-Guy here."

"I hate it when you call me that," mutters O'Neill.

"What?" asks Bradley. "Baby face or Ri-Guy?"

Torres shakes her head. "You two are worse than kids. Maitlan's going to be back any second. We need a plan."

"Maitlan's public persona is as carefully crafted as Bruce Wayne's," I point out. "No one will expect him to come out of the building next door dressed like a jogger, especially one twenty to thirty pounds heavier than Maitlan."

"Agreed," replies Zack, his tone now carrying less of an edge. "But him going to the Boathouse alone seems like an unnecessary risk. There are plenty of tourists in the area. You and I could easily—"

But Maitlan is back and he isn't buying it. "They said no cops. I'm doing this alone."

I can't blame him. But I can't let him go without pointing out something. Something that should be obvious to him in light of our earlier conversation. "Mr. Maitlan, it's common knowledge that your son is missing. We can't rule out the possibility that the man who called doesn't even have your son. Could be he's just taking advantage of the situation, trying to make a quick buck."

"A quick two million bucks," Torres chimes in.

Maitlan is now dressed in running shoes, a pair of ragged sweatpants and a matching hoodie with what appears to be several layers of padding underneath. He pulls the hood up on the jacket. His expression when he looks at me fully reflects that he knows what I'm saying. Still, he doesn't back down. "I'd risk ten times that much if I thought it would get Robby back."

I look to Zack. Part of me thinks we're making a big mistake not filling Torres in on all the possibilities here, but before I can voice my concern, he comes out with one of his own.

"Why ask for two when you can get twenty or more, especially when you could be looking at a life sentence for murder. This doesn't feel right."

Perhaps Maitlan is right: this isn't about money at all, it's about revenge.

An eye for an eye.

"I have to try," Maitlan tells Zack. "If something happens to me, so be it. I have to try."

Zack grabs an earpiece from the table and fits it over Maitlan's ear. "Let's take this one step at a time. You need to make it to the bank and back in an hour."

Maitlan nods. "The money's ready, two million in non-consecutive, used, hundred dollar bills. The bank's just over two miles from here. I can jog there in twenty minutes, maybe a few minutes longer depending on lights and traffic. It'll take what, five minutes to transfer the money into the backpack? They already have a car waiting to take me back. I'll have it drop me around the corner. I can do this." His tone is hopeful.

Zack grasps his shoulder. "You won't be alone. We'll be listening. You do not go directly to the Boathouse. You come back here first. Agreed?"

"Agreed," he says. Then he's gone.

He's barely left the room and Torres is on the phone. "Maitlan's going to be exiting the building— "

Zack grabs her cell. "Belay that." He hangs up.

Torres rounds on him. "You know this isn't a typical ransom drop. Two million is pocket change for a man like Maitlan. Something else is going on here."

Zack nods but doesn't say anything. Instead, he walks over to O'Neill. "Anything from the lab yet?"

After a few keystrokes the agent looks up at Zack. "Ballistics hasn't matched the bullets to anything we have on file. Two weapons. Both 45 Semi-Autos."

"Gang members gun of choice," Zack mutters. "Available at any street corner near you."

O'Neill nods grimly. "The babysitter was shot in the back. Two bullets. Both discharged from the same weapon."

I remember the crime scene tape and the blood stains in the hall. Duplicates of the photos in the dossier are taped to the wall in front of me. My eyes land on the photo of the teen—a beautiful girl who will never graduate from high school, never go to college, never have children of her own.

Another reason to get these guys.

Bradley chimes in, "According to Jackson, she was on the phone with someone when they entered. She screamed. Tried to run. Turns out it was her boyfriend. Phone records show he called back six, seven times and sent a few text messages before dialing 911. Jackson's report came in seven minutes prior. He wasn't out for long, resourceful old bastard. He was able to make it to the kitchen and cut through the cable ties with a knife. The gunmen were in and out in minutes."

The agent leans back in his chair, his expression pensive.

"I don't buy that it's not about the money," he says after a beat. "If they wanted to pop the kid, they could have done it. If they wanted Maitlan, they could have waited and come in later. I say they knew Maitlan was gone and—"

"What if it's not about what they want? What if they're working for someone else?" I ask.

"There's a lot we don't know. But one thing I do know is that there's no risk to Maitlan until he has the money in hand. We're not going to have him followed to the bank. We're going to be waiting for him when he comes out. I'll be waiting for him, standing in for the driver." Zack picks up another earpiece from the table and places it in his own ear. "I'll get him back here safe and sound."

CHAPTER FOUR

"I'm in position." Zack's words fill the room. "Maitlan just went into the bank."

Torres is pacing. "If he's right about the money being ready, he'll be on his way back in just a few minutes. What's the plan, *boss*?"

While Zack was making his way to the bank, I prompted a full review of everything we knew about the case with Torres and her crew. That is, everything except the private conversation Zack and I had with Maitlan in his office. As expected, Maitlan was able to provide Torres with a long list of enemies. A list that has been getting shorter as Torres and her team have worked through it. If the ransom drop goes bad and we reach a dead end, we'll *have* to fill the team in on Maitlan's suspicions. And we will have wasted precious time chasing false leads. I'm uneasy about this, but it's not my story to tell and at this point we don't know what's true.

"I've got Maitlan, we're on our way back. I say we put him in a vest, send him in with a wire," says Zack.

Maitlan's protests come across loud and clear. He didn't expect to see Zack in the car and he's not happy. He may be used to getting his way, but this time Zack cuts him off at the knees.

"Roger, we're in play now. I respect you, but you're out of your depth here. You asked for me to come. I came. Let me do my goddamned job." He doesn't wait for Maitlan's buy-in. Instead he directs a question to Torres. "Agent Torres, you have any other ideas?"

The instant Zack asks her advice, her attitude softens. "You were right about the amount of tourists in that area. It would be easy to station a few agents near the Boathouse. A traditional wire is too risky. It's something they could easily search for."

"Maybe a receiver sewn into the waistband of his trousers." I suggest. "That way if we lose sight, at least we can track him."

"We're just around the corner, should be there in a few. Make it so, Number One," Zack says.

I move closer to the speaker. "I'm glad you finally got the pecking order straight."

In my minds eye I can see his eyes roll. "It's a *Star Trek* reference."

I smile. "I know. I'm just jerking your chain. Your hour is up. Where's Maitlan's closet? I need to find something appropriate for a ransom drop."

As soon as I'm given directions I head for the master suite.

"Emma!" Torres calls out.

"Did we just get the go ahead to position agents there? We don't have much time."

"That's my read. It's a restaurant, right?"

"Yes, and a popular one. Even around that time of day, it will be crowded."

"Do it." I'm off. In less than a minute I've found his closet and grabbed another pair of sweatpants. I search through the drawers in the adjoining bathroom for a sewing kit. I score on the second try; the middle drawer is filled with miniature shampoo bottles and soaps from hotels, and a half-dozen tiny sewing kits. I grab one and race back to the conference room, trying not to think too hard about why a multi-billionaire hoards hotel grooming products.

The guys have already returned.

Maitlan skins off the hoodie then, one-by-one, he pulls the extra sweaters over his head, piling them on top of the backpack at his feet. The two-million-dollar ransom.

Zack wastes no time. After a glance at the clock on the wall, he straps Maitlan into a bulletproof vest. "You have forty minutes to make it to the Boathouse."

Torres slides the receiver across the table. "State of the art GPS. It's no bigger than a quarter and flexible. Sewn into the waistband, it will be undetectable."

I'm doing my best to thread the fucking needle from the sewing kit, compliments of the Ritz in Atlanta, and failing miserably. Torres pulls out a Swiss Army knife, grabs the pair of sweats and after a few swipes has ripped open the seem. "Give me that," she says. "We don't have all day. Looks like it's been a while since you made a Halloween costume."

"Halloween costume?" I hand over the pair of sweats and the kit from the Ritz.

"My daughter wants to be a ninja. My son a dinosaur." She threads the needle on the first try. I watch as it dips in and out of the fabric. "The dinosaur costume is going to be a bitch. I started on it last weekend."

It's the first personal thing Torres has shared. I smile.

Zack makes one final adjustment to the vest then pats Maitlan on the chest. "As soon as Torres is finished, you need to change into these sweats. We'll be able to track your every move. If you don't want a tail, you have to make this concession."

Maitlan pulls the last sweater back over his head. "You're not leaving me a choice."

There's a pause while the two men stare at each other.

"No, sir, I'm not," Zack replies, handing him the hoodie. "Trust me."

Finally, Maitlan nods. "I do."

Torres hands him the pair of sweatpants she's been working on. She flexes the waistband. "See? It's undetectable."

He takes them from her and kicks off his running shoes.

"Let's get a map of the area up where we can see it," Zack asks. There's a large flat screen at the end of the conference room. It takes Torres less time to get the images of Central Park up on the screen than it takes Maitlan to strip off his ragged sweats and step into the other pair.

Zack steps up to the monitor to get a closer look. "We need to map out your route." He points to a flashing red dot. "This is you right here."

Maitlan slips his shoes back on, laces them up. Then he joins Zack and begins to trace a route with his finger. "I'll go back up Fifth Avenue to the 72nd Street entrance. It's the most direct route to the Boathouse. Should take me twenty-five minutes."

Zack nods. "Okay. Better get going. We'll follow you on screen."

And on the ground, I think. Certain that as soon as Maitlan leaves the board will light up with agents stationed in and around the Boathouse.

Maitlan once again slips the hood of his sweatshirt up to cover his head and without a backward glance or another word, he grabs the backpack and heads out the door.

I watch the dot as it slowly moves. See a half-dozen blue ones light up. I don't like having to watch from the sidelines, feeling so useless. Zack seems to like it even less.

"These are ours?" he asks, finger sweeping over the screen, connecting the dots.

Torres nods, eyes glued to the map.

"What do you think the chances are this is a legitimate drop?" I ask.

Zack shrugs. "Your guess is as good as mine. The fact that this is happening in broad daylight is bothering me."

"There's a lot about this bothering me," I throw in.

"If it is legit, chances are it won't happen at the Boathouse," continues Zack. "They have to know a two-hour window would allow us enough time to get our people in place. This probably isn't the final location. Do we have eyes in the sky?" he asks.

Torres shakes her head. "Only the ones on the ground right now. There's a chopper on standby, but I'm keeping it out of the immediate airspace. Let's open up com."

"We're on speaker," says Bradley.

I grab another cup of coffee, sink into a chair, listen as they check in. If Maitlan is wrong about Eve, and the money is really what the kidnappers are after, Robby may be back home before the day is over. I wish I was more confident that was the case. But I can feel it in my bones. There will be another call. To think this will be it...that the kidnapper will show up to exchange the money for the boy is unrealistic. There are too many people around. Too many ways for a cop to be hidden in plain sight.

Finally, a message comes through from the field agent closest to the tree. She identifies herself as Perez and tells us that shortly after Maitlan's arrival, his cell phone rang. He has it to his ear. He's listening.

Zack places a hand on Bradley's shoulder. "Patch into his cell phone," he says.

Perez's voice comes back. "Target just tossed his cell in the trash. Looks like a burner was taped to the underside of the lid. Target's pocketed it and is on the move. I can follow with the stroller."

"Do it." Zack joins Torres who's tracking Maitlan on the flat screen. "But keep a safe distance."

I join them as Maitlan's indicator heads down Park Drive.

Another agent's voice comes through. "It looks

like Target is heading back toward the 72nd Street entrance"

We watch as he turns west at the junction instead of east. In a few minutes he's made another turn. A crackling message comes through.

"I think Target's heading for the Bandshell."

I tap the location of the Bandshell on the screen. It's closer than the Boathouse was to Maitlan's penthouse. "Can we get a couple agents in position there? These two look close."

"Perfetti and Campbell," Torres says. "They're on bikes." She speaks into her headset. "Do you have Target in sight?"

"Target in sight," one of the agents replies. "We'll be passing Target any minute."

We watch as Perez falls back a bit and the other two agents take the lead. Within a minute they're in front of Maitlan and heading for the Bandshell. The same agent is still keeping up a running commentary. "There are a few street performers in the area, a small crowd around them. We should be able to blend in." A minute passes before they lay eyes on him. "Target's in front of the Bandshell. A call is coming in." There's a brief silence, then, "Target's heading back on Park Drive, looks like he's going south."

"Perez, do you have the Target?" Zack asks. "How is he holding up?"

"Not good from the looks of it. That backpack has to be getting pretty heavy by now. Target is sweating profusely. Probably part nerves, part exhaustion."

"Not to mention the extra layers of clothing." I

look over at Torres. "Where do you think he's heading?"

"Not sure," she replies. "He'll be passing the Visitors Center soon. If he doesn't stop there, it might be the carousel."

I feel a sudden spark of hope. "If there is going to be a swap, that would be a logical place to do it. The place is always teeming with kids. Robby wouldn't be conspicuous."

Torres quirks an eyebrow but doesn't reply. I can tell she isn't feeling the same burst of optimism I am. Zack, too, remains silent, stoic.

I check the clock on the wall. Maitlan's been gone well over an hour and he's been on the move most of that time. "It's going to be dusk soon."

Zack starts to reply when Perez interrupts. "Target is past the Visitor's Center. I'm betting on the Carousel. Can you get another agent there?"

"No one's close enough. It's on you. Looks like he's coming up on it now. Any sign of Robby?"

"Shit. Target is on the phone again. I'm hanging back. Target's yelling in the phone. It's attracting attention. People are stopping, staring. Should I move in?"

Torres speaks up. "No. Not yet. He'll snap out of it. He's not a stranger to pressure. He knows what's at stake."

"You're right, boss," says Perez, "Target's jogging south again. Toward Seventh Avenue. Wait. There's some kind of demonstration going on. I'm losing sight of him."

Zack's strikes the wall with his fist.

Torres' eyes are fixed on the screen. "He just

moved past the Seventh Street entrance. He's headed for Broadway. Get through the crowd, try to catch up."

I don't realize I've been holding my breath until it catches in my throat. "They're playing with him," I whisper. "Playing with us. How long can Perez keep this up?"

"She's a marathon runner," replies Torres. "I'm more worried about Maitlan."

"His adrenaline's got to be through the roof," adds Zack.

The tension in the room builds along with the pressure in my chest. All the optimism I felt about the carousel being the natural place to make an exchange is gone. If I'm right, Robby won't be waiting for him at the next location, either.

"Target's slowing down. Looks like he's pausing to catch his breath. Another call just came in. He's doing a three-sixty. Something they said must have given him the impression they're close. Watching. I've been with him for quite a while. I think I should break away."

"We have a car close to Columbus Circle. An agent's being dropped off, Bao Nguyen, do you see him?" asks Torres.

"Not yet. Target's crossing the Circle. I'll cross with him then move past to the café across the street. Is Nguyen close?"

A new man's voice comes across. "I'm in position."

"You should see him across the circle at twelve o'clock, dark suit and overcoat, shopping bags in hand," Torres replies.

"Looking very metro-sexual, Nguyen," Perez teases.

"Bite me."

"Target's waiting for a break in the traffic." Perez's tone is once again focused, professional. "I'm approaching. I'll head over to the coffee shop after we cross."

"Boy or girl?" Suddenly we recognize Maitlan's voice.

"Girl," replies Perez. "Trying to run off that baby fat."

They must be jogging side by side. The red and blue dots are moving in tandem across the screen. The fountain and Columbus Monument is ahead of them.

"How old?" asks Maitland, sounding a little breathless.

"Four months."

Torres breaks in. "Wave toward the coffee chop as if you see someone you're planning on meeting, then head in that direction."

We watch Perez break to the left. The dots separate.

Nguyen picks up the narrative. "Target's on the phone again. He's on the walkway that leads over the fountain to the monument. He's looking back at Perez. I'm going to get a bit closer."

We wait. For a moment or two there's nothing but silence.

"Target's removing the backpack. Holding it. He's approaching a trash receptacle by the wall. Looks like this is the drop."

We hear the ringing of a cell phone as the two

dots on the map converge, then Nguyen's moves past. "Wait, he's looking back at Perez again. Maybe he made her. Shit! Target is running toward the coffee shop."

Maitlan doesn't get far.

A blast rips through the line, filling the room with a sound loud enough to rattle all of us.

"Nguyen? Perez?" Torres yells. "What the fuck just happened?"

We hear sirens, screaming. We watch as the dot representing Perez runs toward the chaos. Her breathing is heavy, erratic. "Are you all right?" she yells over the din.

Maitlan's voice comes through. "What?"

"Don't move," she says, then she's on the run again. "He's shaken, got tossed from the force of the blast, but he seems all right. I'm checking on Nguyen."

Suddenly her voice cuts off. There's just the sound of ragged breaths and sirens, then sobs. Perez pulls herself together. "Agent down. He's unconscious but alive."

"Thank god," Torres whispers.

"Looks like Target's on the move. Intercept," Zack orders.

"Too late, He's in a Taxi," Perez replies. "Shall I pursue?"

"Stay with Nguyen." Zack tells her. Then, to Torres, "Get the chopper up. With the explosion, there's bound to be several around the area already." Whatever else Zack was going to say is interrupted by the ring of his phone.

"What cell are you on?" His tone is abrupt, all

business. "Good. Toss the one they gave you out the window." He turns to Torres, "It's Maitlan. He's in a taxi. Can the guys in the chopper see if he's being followed?"

She speaks into her headset, listens, then shakes her head. "Too early to tell. We should pick him up."

Zack nods. "Have Ahmed drive you to MoMa. I'll meet you there in five." He hangs up, heads for the door. "Be back in fifteen."

"Zack!" I call out. "Do you think they wanted Maitlan dead?"

He turns back, expression grim. "Either that, or they wanted him to know it's not about the money," he replies before taking off.

Torres' voice is husky with anger. A member of her team is injured. The seriousness of his condition, unknown. "There was never going to be an exchange. What the hell do these fuckers want?"

"An eye for an eye," I murmur to myself.

CHAPTER FIVE

Torres and I are there to meet Zack and Maitlan when they step out of the elevator. Maitlan has one scrape on his chin and another on his left cheek from being thrown to the ground during the blast. Despite having had time to recover in the taxi, his breathing is still a bit labored.

"Are you all right?" I ask.

"No." His tone is clipped, angry. "I'm not all right."

Maitlan moves past us and down the stairs. Seconds later I hear a door slam.

"He needs a little space," says Zack, motioning us toward the kitchen. "And we need to talk."

"Shouldn't we be debriefing with the entire team?" asks Torres.

"Not yet. Maybe not ever," Zack replies. "Roger wasn't looking at Perez. Right before the trash can blew, he saw a woman he recognized in the coffee shop across the street."

"That's why he started running toward the café?" Torres asks.

He nods. "Maitlan and this woman have a history."

Torres' expression says she's trying to work a puzzle with missing pieces. "The kind of history that might motivate her to kidnap his son?"

Zack doesn't hesitate. "Possibly. By the time Maitlan recovered from the blast she was gone."

Torres' voice rises. "Why the hell wasn't she on the list?"

"Were there any women on the list he gave you?"

"No."

Zack shrugs. "Man like Roger Maitlan, I'm sure he's made enemies of dozens of women. He probably just dismissed them out of hand, not seeing them as..."

"A valid threat," Torres finishes, her exasperation growing. I recognize the signs—tense jaw, stiff shoulders. "Misogynistic prick."

Zack says nothing to alter her impression. "The circumstances are delicate."

She throws each word at him like she's hurling a knife. "Delicate? Is that what I'm supposed to tell Nguyen's wife? Not to mention the others who were injured?"

The tension in the room is mounting. "Whatever Roger Maitlan may be, he's a victim, a father whose son's life is in danger. Let's not forget that." I turn to Torres, "I realize you almost lost an agent today, and I'm sorry for that. If this woman is responsible, then let's nail her ass. You're angry, I understand that, too. But channel that anger. Let's keep things professional."

After a long moment of silence Torres nods. "You're right." She turns to Zack, "I want to know everything he told you about this woman. Who is she? What does she have against Maitlan?"

Zack turns to me. Our eyes lock. He doesn't have to ask. I know what he wants. Zack wants me to use my gift to find out if we can trust Torres, if it's safe to reveal Maitlan's suspicions about Devlin to her.

"Maybe you should go check on Mr. Maitlan," I suggest. "Then we can regroup in the conference room for a debriefing in five."

"How about we begin the debriefing now?" Torres is feeling impatient. I can't blame her. We all are.

Zack makes no motion to leave. If I lower my shields enough to extract the truth, my other innate magic will also seep through—my powers of seduction. Zack knows it. He's experienced it. I vowed he'd never be subjected to that temptation again. I may not like the tension between Zack and me, but at least now he's alive.

And what of Demeter? Finding the missing is my penance. Doing it well, my promised salvation. But using my gifts? Risking attention? That comes at a price, a knowing reduction of whatever good will I've managed to build with the vindictive goddess.

"Have you ever heard of Elysium?" Zack asks.

He's looking at me when he asks the question. It's the question he wants me to ask Torres.

I've been playing this game of scales for so long, I don't know how to keep track anymore. Last night, before it all unraveled, I thought I was closer than I'd ever been to ending my sentence. Now? If Eve really is involved with Robby's kidnapping, we need to go after her. We need to know if we can trust Torres. Seems the decision is out of my hands. All I can think of is the little boy who is missing.

"Elysium?" I repeat. "I don't believe so"

Torres frowns. "I take it we're not talking about the Matt Damon movie?"

I begin the process of lowering my shields and tapping into my power. The temperature in the room climbs a few degrees. A wind rises up within me. I tamp it down. Emotions in the room are already running high. I need to stay in control, work my magic with calculated measure. Zack's nostrils flare, undoubtedly detecting my change in scent, the subtle, perfumed breeze that always accompanies exposure of my true self. A delicate yet complex blend of white floral layered atop citrus begins to permeate the room. The scent is what betrayed me, or should I say revealed me, two nights ago.

It had been six months since I'd carelessly left a shirt I'd worn behind at Zack's beach house. It smelled of sex and something else. Something that even with his training and his beast Zack couldn't recognize or reconcile—until we made love. Until, unguarded, I once again broke free. That's when he put it together, that we'd been lovers before. That I was the one, who had worn his shirt, slept in his bed. And that somehow I'd taken those memories from him.

Zack doesn't glance my way. Instead he stays focused on Torres. "No, we're talking about a place, here, in New York."

I push what happened between Zack and me to

the back of my mind. Concentrate on where we are, the here and now. On what our goal is. On finding a little boy. I squeeze my eyes shut for a moment to regain focus.

Maitlan's kitchen is an homage to stainless steel and granite. The air around me stirs, but there's little evidence of it in this room. No drapes fluttering. No papers ruffling. A strand of hair escapes the coil at the nape of my neck and drifts in front of my eyes. I quickly tuck it back behind my ear. There's no need to draw this out. All I need to do is repeat the question. "You're a local. Do *you* know anything about a place, here, in New York, called Elysium?"

Torres blinks. Her face is flush, her pupils expand. "No, but the Big Apple's a big place."

"Might Bradley or O'Neill?"

"I doubt it. O'Neill's lived in DC since he graduated from high school. Bradley's from Philly."

We have our answer, the chance that any of our team members could be linked to Elysium or Eve Devlin are essentially nil. I rein in my magic and rebuild the walls before turning to Zack. Our eyes meet for only a fraction of a second before he turns away. But in that moment I see a flash of blue, the eyes of his beast.

Zack goes to the refrigerator and pulls out a coke. He takes a long draw, as if swallowing down whatever effect being exposed once again to my powers awakened in him.

I fill in the moment of silence by asking a question. "So, what is this Elysium?"

Zack buries his hands in his pockets. "It's a...

club owned by a woman named Eve Devlin. Mr. Maitlan was a member of that club. Two weeks ago Eve's daughter, Amanda, committed suicide there. Eve blames him for Amanda's death."

Torres' eyes narrow. "So, this isn't about money."

"It's about revenge." Maitlan's standing in the doorway. He looks every bit as worn and defeated as his tone indicates. "You've told *everyone*."

"Only the people in this room know, Roger."

"And what we know is precious little," Torres snaps.

Maitlan rubs his hand over his face. "Do any of you honestly think my son is still alive?"

"We have no reason to believe otherwise." I tell him, and I believe it. "If this is about revenge, then Devlin has nothing against your son. It's you she wants to hurt, right? If Robby was dead, she'd want you to know it, see you suffer."

"An eye for an eye—a daughter for a son," Zack says quietly.

Torres folds her arms in front of her chest. "Mr. Maitlan, I think it's time you fill us in on everything you know."

Maitlan looks to Zack.

Zack gives him a nod of encouragement. "It's your story and it's time to tell it. And Roger? Don't leave anything out."

Maitlan has gone upstairs to shower and change. We're all sitting around the conference table turned command center. Bradley and O'Neill have been debriefed. Torres checks her watch. "I need to go to the hospital. Speak to Nguyen's wife."

"How is he?" I ask.

"Still in a comma," she says.

Bradley winces. "Kids?"

"Three." Torres slides on her coat. "The ATF has taken over the scene at the park. If there's anything there to find, they'll find it."

"But will they find it in time?" asks O'Neill.

I turn my attention to the large screen, where there's a photo of Eve, and rub my temples. I'm tired and hungry and frustrated. "Considering the distance between Maitlan and the café and the fact that it was only Maitlan who saw her, do you think we could get a warrant for surveillance? Obviously, she's not working alone. Best-case scenario, we get evidence that she's behind a sizable conspiracy. Minimally we can build a case for the host of other crimes being committed at Elysium."

"You're suggesting we bring in a tact team to plant bugs?" asks Bradley.

I shake my head. "Considering the timeline and the fact that we know Devlin has law enforcement in her pocket, I was thinking we'd handle it ourselves. If we could get a judge to sign off on a covert—"

"But which judge can we trust?" O'Neill asks.

Torres pulls a card out of her purse and slides it across the table in his direction. "This one."

Zack picks it up. "Anita Lopez?"

Torres smiles. "My aunt. Now, you the rest of you can put your heads together and figure out how we're going to get in and out."

"That's not going to be easy." Maitlan is hovering in the doorway. Fresh from the shower, his hair still wet. You can't just walk into Eve's club. It's private. Very private. You have to be sponsored by a member. And there's a vetting process. Eve doesn't take chances—she's not about to risk everything because an undercover cop sneaks in and discovers she's serving more than alcohol."

"But her reputation for being able to satisfy customers is important to her." I pause, collecting my thoughts. "What about her employees? Any way we could convince one of them to help?"

Maitlan pulls his wallet from his back pocket. In it, there's a slip of paper. "Maybe. One of the girls slipped me this as I was leaving the last time. It's her number. I haven't called it. I chose a place like that for a reason. Attachments are not what I want."

"Give it here." I hold out my hand. "What's her name?"

"She wrote Jennifer under the number," he says nonchalantly. Then, "But I usually call her Mistress Darkness." He pulls his hand back. The slip of paper is out of reach. "What are you going to ask her?"

"If she's working, I'm going to offer her an obscene amount of money to get sick at the last minute and send me to Elysium in her stead—her BFF who just moved here from Los Angeles."

"She always works Fridays. Starts at eight." Maitlan pauses, looks me up and down. "You understand what Mistress, um, Jennifer does?"

I rise from my chair and stride toward him with purpose, gaze unwavering. He doesn't flinch as I swiftly close the space between us and snatch the slip of paper from his hand. "In general, yes. For you, specifically, I can guess."

Torres is looking at me as if I've lost my mind. "No offense, but you are one of the most buttoned up agents I've ever met. Even dressed in leather and holding a whip, I don't see you passing yourself off as a professional dominatrix."

"No offense," I counter, feeling more than a bit offended. "But you don't really know me."

None of the men in the room weighs in with an opinion.

I turn to Zack. "You're in charge and you *know* I can pull this off."

There's no hesitation. "She can do it," he says, putting the question to rest. Then he looks at Maitlan. "So, how do we get Emma past Eve? Based on what you've said, I doubt she's going to let someone who she doesn't know just waltz in and substitute."

I answer before Maitlan can. "The timing is going to have to be just right and we prey on Eve's need to satisfy her customers. Maitlan says Jennifer starts at eight. We have her call in sick five minutes before her shift is supposed to start. I show up a few minutes after that. I can be..." I pause, holding Zack's gaze with my own. "Very persuasive."

"Say you do get in, how are you going to sneak away from your client and get into Eve's office?"

"That's where you come in," I tell Torres. "Robby's story is all over the news. After what happened in the park today, you can say you're expanding the investigation, interviewing everyone who knows Maitlan. His financial records show he's a member of her private club, the legitimate club, so you're stopping by to ask her a few questions about anyone he may have been in contact with in the days before Robby's kidnapping."

"So, I draw her out of the office long enough for you to get inside and plant a bug?"

"Actually, I imagine she'll have me brought to her office as soon as I show up. I can plant the bug then. When you arrive, if you can get her to take you into her office and keep her there for ten to fifteen minutes, that would give me enough time to get into her private apartment."

"It could work," Bradley says.

O'Neill adds, "And right now, it's the best plan we've got."

"What time do you want me there?" asks Torres

I mull it over for a moment. "Eight fifteen."

Maitlan takes the slip of paper from my hand and then heads across the hall, back toward his office. "I'll call Mistress Darkness from my office. If we're going to be offering her an obscene amount of *my* money, I want to be negotiating." When he reaches the door he turns around just long enough to ask, "Whom should she tell them to expect?"

"Domina Sirena," I reply before turning to Torres. "Any idea where I can get a latex catsuit and a whip."

"Honey, I'm a single mother with two kids under six. Closest thing I could get you would be my orange tabby and a can of Redi-whip," she says with a smile. "Text me the address, I'll be there at eight fifteen sharp."

I feel Zack's hand on my elbow. "Let's ask Mistress Darkness."

CHAPTER SIX

I survey the pile of shopping bags that adorn the king-sized bed in the guest room Maitlan has assigned to me. There's an adjoining bathroom that links to a second guest room on the other side. The one assigned to Zack.

"Looks like quite a haul."

I turn at the sound of Zack's voice.

He's leaning against the doorjamb. His pose appears casual, relaxed. But I've worked with him long enough to know there's something about the mission that's bothering him. I scoop up the bag of make-up and a flat-iron.

"I need to begin the transformation. It may take a while."

He steps back into the bathroom so that I can enter. But he doesn't leave. Instead he perches on the end of the large marble tub. "I've been thinking about something Torres said."

I plug in the flat iron. My hair is naturally thick and wavy. Tonight it will be straight, worn in a ponytail high on my head. I need my overall look to be striking, severe. I dump out the bag of make-up. Pick up a tube of lipstick, Moulin

Rouge. It's a vibrant red. "What's that?"

"About you being the buttoned up, librarian type."

Of course Zack has seen another side of me. Our eyes connect in the mirror.

He clears his throat. "I have an observation. And a question."

I pick up the flat iron and begin the process of straightening my hair. "Fire away."

He scratches the back of his head. "I don't know much about your kind." There's an uncharacteristic hesitation. "But I'd like to think I've grown to know a bit about you. Torres is right, in a way. You go to great lengths day to day to…" There's a longer pause this time. Finally he finds the word he's searching for. "Hide."

I say nothing. He's yet to ask the question. I wait and continue working on my waves, straightening the long cascade of locks into a smooth, shiny dark sheet.

"You're so reserved most of the time. But I've seen you let go and when that happens…" Color rises to his cheeks. He stands, comes to lean against the vanity. "You're going to be heading into a sexually charged situation. You're going to be alone. I need to know if this is going to be a problem for you."

I finish with the last bit of hair, quickly pulling it into a topknot, letting the length spill down my back before facing him. "I've been playing this game for a very long time. I know the dangers of letting go. That's why I so rarely let it happen. This performance is all about control. I can handle it. In fact, you might say I'm uniquely qualified for it."

He nods, seemingly satisfied. Yet he still doesn't leave.

I start in on the make-up. Concealer for under the eyes, base, powder to set it. There's blush, three different eye shadows of varying shades of gray, along with liquid eyeliner and mascara. Zack watches quietly as I use a variety of sponges and brushes to create a flawless canvas before beginning to paint. It feels intimate, and his presence is strangely comforting. Maybe it's the fact that the tension between us has defused. That with Robby's life at stake and a job to focus on we're back on even keel. Maybe it's the fact that the conversation is an honest one and that since the moment I bespelled him, took away his memories of our affair, there hasn't really been a true and real conversation between us.

I blot my lipstick and then add a touch of gloss. "Now for wardrobe."

I walk back into the bedroom, flip the cover off a large shoebox containing an impressive pair of leather boots. There's a second box. I strip away the tissue paper to reveal a cat suit of exceptional quality. The collar is high. The racerback cut is sure to reveal my wings, or should I say the markings where my wings used to be. That's something I hadn't counted on. I slide the catch down on the zipper. It runs from collar to crotch.

I step out of my shoes. Begin to unbutton my blouse.

"I'm still here you know."

My back is to him. The sound comes from the

direction of the bathroom. This time it's me who shrugs. "I know," I say, removing my shirt. Unfastening the catch on my trousers. We've spent hours exploring one another's bodies. It's seems silly to act the modest coquette now. "Question is why?"

I'm down to my bra and panties.

When he replies I can tell that he hasn't moved. He's keeping a measure of distance between us. "Thought you might need help with the getup. That zipper's going to be a bitch."

I look over my shoulder. He holds up both hands. "Strictly professional."

I don't invite him in.

The bra and panties fall to the floor, then I turn around and sit on the edge of the bed, in all my naked glory. I don't look up.

"I could ask one of the other guys," he says, his voice quiet.

I shake my head. Feel my hair bob back and forth as it brushes against the skin of my back. I step into the legs, then stand, pulling the suit up, over my torso and pushing my hands through the armholes.

"Don't bother. You'll do," I tell him, turning back around and sweeping my hair over one shoulder so it doesn't catch in the zip. "You may enter, dog."

It takes him only a few quick strides to reach me, to have my hair in his fist. His eyes, flashing blue, connect with mine. "Being submissive isn't something I play at. I don't need a mommy to spank me. You want someone to practice on before you go inside? Practice on Roger." With that he reaches around behind me, slides his hand down between my legs to grab hold of the zipper. His thumb brushes across my clit, and an involuntary hiss escapes my lips. I remember a time that, thanks to Liz's spell, Zack never will. A time when I'd wanted him, needed him, so much I'd practically begged. His eyes hold mine steadily as the fabric comes together over my ass, my back, my neck.

I pick up a boot. "Do you suppose I could get Roger to lick these?"

He swipes it from my hand, then plants his other in the middle of my chest and gives me a little push so that I fall back onto the bed. "I suppose you could get any man to do anything," he replies, plucking the boot's stuffing out and dropping it onto the floor.

"Even you?" I ask. Holding out one foot, inviting him to slip it on.

He obliges with a sad smile. "*I'm* pissed at you. Remember?"

My second foot pops out, ready to be sheathed. "What I remember, is you agreeing to put that aside for now." I reach back on the bed, my fingers curl around the piece that completes the outfit, a Hermes riding crop. Nothing but the best for Maitlan's Domina. A flick of my wrist and it snaps against my leather clad leg. "Are we all set with the equipment?"

Zack nods. "The bag's ready. A few select items no Domina would leave home without inside the main compartment. Surveillance equipment stowed away underneath the false bottom. And, I called in an unofficial favor. Thermal imaging reveals no children in the building. Maitlan was right. If Eve does have Robby, she's not holding him at Elysium. Jennifer's ready to make the call."

"Looks like I'm off," I say, heading for the door.

Just as I open it he surprises me with, "I'm going with you."

I stop dead in my tracks. "I've got this, Zack. Besides, there's no way they would let you in. You heard Roger—"

"Not me, my wolf. We have a body count. You're going in completely unarmed." He waves in my direction. "You can't even wear any protective gear. I can shift and recover from a bullet. You can't. Think of me as a prop."

"A prop."

He smiles a bit sheepishly. "You know, you're so bad you've tamed a big bad wolf."

My hands move to my hips. "You're confusing as hell, you know that?"

"I prefer to think of myself as complicated."

"You're telling me you can shift at will?" It's a rare skill, and one Zack's never mentioned. It's something only the strongest Were's can do.

"Handy, right?" he replies.

"You can control the beast?"

"One hundred percent, with the exception of that pesky leg humping problem."

I roll my eyes. "Let's go." I turn to leave. Once again, he stops me.

"Emma!"

"What?"

"One more thing. I'd prefer it if you didn't watch me change."

I approach him. "You've watched me change."

"True. But this is different. It's painful and grisly. Once you see it, you'll never be able to forget there's a monster inside of the man."

Suddenly he looks vulnerable.

My hand reaches up to cup the side of his face. He doesn't pull away. "There's a monster inside of all of us. You have the privilege of being better acquainted with yours than most."

He takes my hand. Lowers it. "Say you understand. That you won't fight me on this."

"I understand," I assure him. "I won't fight you on this."

There's a knock on the door. I turn to find Maitlan. He's giving me the once-over. His eyes hold more than curiosity. Before he says anything, Zack steps forward. "Were you able to get any sleep?"

Maitlan shakes his head. "Tried for the past hour. Not a wink. Where are we?"

"I have the results of the thermal scan. You're right. Robby is not being held in the club. We got the warrant. The plan is the same, Emma will offer to take over Jennifer's clients for the night. Torres will come in to distract Eve. Emma will then use the opportunity to get into Eve's office and apartment and place the bugs. We're ready to go."

"We?" asks Maitlan.

Zack pulls a set of keys from his jacket. "I'm going to drive her."

* * * *

Maitlan's directions put the club in the middle of Manhattan. Even with traffic, it's a simple commute.

In twenty minutes we're pulling past the address and driving into a nearby alley between two closed businesses. Although the sign above our parking spot threatens to tow away any car, with the exception of those belonging to patrons, there's little risk of that with government plates.

He shuts off the ignition. "My costume's in the glove compartment."

I pop it open; pull out a studded collar and leather leash.

"Once we're inside, take me off leash. That way I'll be able to maneuver more easily should something go awry." He flips off the interior lights before opening the driver's door.

"Nothing's going to go awry," I assure him.

We're enveloped in darkness. I can barely see the outline of his body. A pair of shoes gets tossed into the front seat. Trousers follow, then the remainder of his clothing. Finally, he tosses me the keys. "The alley up ahead that runs perpendicular butts up against the back of Elysium. I say we take it instead of the main street, it will allow us easy access to the side entrance Jennifer told us about."

"Agreed," I slip the keys inside my bag, step out of the SUV. My eyes are adjusting somewhat. I can see that Zack's no longer alongside the car.

It rained a short while ago. The streets are wet. Manhattan is abuzz. I look back to see cars whizzing by in front of the alley. But above the din of the city, I hear the cracking of bone. My stomach churns. I step closer to the sound. Hear the tearing of sinew. There's a faint outline of a dumpster up ahead. I know what's happening behind it—a human skeleton is being mangled. Ripped apart. Joints severed and reshaped. Muscle shredded, then knit back together. Until, finally in an explosion of blood and gore—the wolf emerges. The monster inside the man. I turn back around, try to block out the sounds of what I know must be a torturous transformation, focus on the traffic whizzing by. Then, quite suddenly, I feel something wet against the back of my hand. Hear a gentle whimper. The headlights of a car in the alley across the street shine on us. Bright light reflects off white fur. Zack's wolf is beautiful, its head reaches almost to my waist. Reflexively I reach down and run my hand over its coat, which is full and thick, the edges of its ears are darker, as is a patch between his eyes, a section around his haunches. Those areas appear more of a light grey. But it's the eyes that catch my true attention and hold it. They're eyes I've seen before, as blue as an arctic sky.

The car pulls out into traffic. Once again we're shrouded in darkness. I fasten the collar around his neck, don't bother with the leash. It's dropped into my bag. "We didn't discuss what I should call you," I say softly, lifting its head. "How about Cerberus?"

The wolf tilts its head as if considering the matter. I start walking. Cerberus remains by my side, vigilant, alert. "Because your loyalty rivals the Hellhounds' that guard Hades gates. Let's go, partner, this is going to be one entrance Eve Devlin will never forget."

CHAPTER SEVEN

With Cerberus by my side I ring the bell to the side entrance. It's nondescript, no address, not even a light overhead or alongside. We have to wait only a few seconds before the door opens. The brightness that suddenly floods the streets makes me take a step back. I shield my eyes.

"I take it you're the new Domina?" A man with the stature of a body-builder fills the door. He's dressed in a perfectly tailored tuxedo. He's obviously expecting me, but his eyes reflect surprise then trouble upon seeing the wolf. "We don't allow dogs inside."

Cerberus bares his teeth.

"He doesn't come in, I don't come in." I glance down and in a clipped tone say, "Behave yourself."

The wolf sits, lowers his head in deference to my command.

"We're a team," I add.

"Miss Eve isn't going to like this," he says with a frown, then steps back so we can enter.

I flash him a brazen smile. "She's going to love what we can do for her clients."

The man leads us down a dark hall, through a

door, then up a short flight of stairs. At the top, he pauses before sweeping aside a thick, velvet curtain. On the other side is a reception area with a hostess stand and a coatroom. The floors are marbled, the walls wood paneled. To the left is a room with a long bar, reminiscent of one I used to frequent at the Waldorf back when I last worked in New York. That seems like a lifetime ago.

It *was* a lifetime ago.

The bar area is filled with leather sofas and chairs. Large oriental rugs warm the room. There are bookcases and racks containing newspapers, undoubtedly from around the world. There's a bartender behind the bar. Two gentlemen occupy chairs, one smoking a pipe. Beyond that I glimpse a dining room, its tables covered with crisp white cloths, fine china, and delicate crystal.

"This way," my guide says, leading me past the hostess.

The lithe blonde barely spares me a glance. Her attention is drawn instead to my wolf. She bends over burying her face in the top of his head, giving him a scratch behind his ears and a nice view of her ample breasts.

"Cerberus," I say. "Come!"

He breaks away and follows at my heels. "Speaking of names, I didn't get yours," I say to the back of my escort.

"Nigel," he replies.

"Seriously?" I ask him.

He pauses in front of a large double door. "You can call me Duke." He raps twice, then turns the knob.

In the center of the office, a woman sits behind a Queen Anne desk made of mahogany, her face obscured by a fall of dark hair, paging through what looks like an old ledger. Is that the ledger Maitlan wanted Zack to steal? Perhaps. She doesn't bother to look up when we enter. Which is fine by me. It gives me a chance to check out the room. The walls are a dark green. Tall windows, framed in taupe velvet, look out onto the street. Two chairs in matching upholstery are positioned in front of the desk.

"Take a seat," she says absently, turning her attention toward a computer monitor. "Domina Sirena, is it?"

Finally I have her full attention.

"Cerberus, lay," I say softly.

The wolf curls up at the base of my feet.

Eve rises. Hands on her desk, she leans over to take in the view. "Mistress Darkness said nothing about a dog."

"Wolf," I say. "I can assure you, he's completely under my control. A model of obedience."

The dark hair is sprinkled with gray. Her face round, cheeks full. The makeup is subtle. The clothing is classic, black slacks and turtleneck sweater. Eve Devlin isn't a flamboyant madam, dripping sex. Nor is she a glamorous society woman. She's all business. Her steel blue eyes fix upon me with the intensity of a laser. Her lips press into a frown.

"Is he really a full-blood wolf?"

I nod. "Arctic wolf."

"You say he's tame, yet you've named him after a Hellhound," she says.

"I said he's obedient, within my control. I wouldn't call him tame." I reach down, give Cerberus a scratch behind the ears. Her eyes follow my left hand. I reach into the top of one boot with my right and palm the bug.

Eve takes her seat once again. "So, you and Jennifer met where?"

"Sarah Lawrence," I say, matter-of-factly. "We both majored in anthropology."

Her face remains stoic. "Is that right?"

I cross my legs, lean back in my chair. "I went on and got my masters in archeology at UCLA. Just accepted a day job as a conservationist at the Natural History Museum."

She leans forward in her chair. "And yet you're here."

"Living in the city is expensive and I have school loans to pay. Plus..." My eyes connect with hers. "I enjoy the work."

She picks up a pen. "Your real name?"

"Patrice Carney," I say.

It's scribbled into the book.

"Address?"

I ramble off Jennifer's.

The book closes with a snap.

"Are you a police officer?"

"Yes, I'm an FBI agent." My tone is flat as I climb to my feet. I position one hand on her desk, use the opportunity to curl the fingers of the other underneath the top and place the bug. "Cerberus here is my partner. An ancestor of his was cursed. Now three nights a week he turns into a wolf. I'd show you our ID's, but we didn't count on needing them to get into your dungeon. Are we going to do this or not?"

For the first time, Eve smiles. Her eyes roam my body. "I like you. Your first client is waiting downstairs."

She picks up the phone on her desk, punches a few numbers. "Nigel, please come back and escort Domina Sirena to level two, dungeon six." She hands me an iPad. "Louis is new. Here's his profile. You also have a nine o'clock. Since you're late, I suggest you give Louis something a little special. You'll leave that with Nigel at the end of the night. He'll pay you. In cash of course. Any questions."

I pick up my bag and head for the door, iPad in hand, wolf at my heels. "Not my first rodeo," I reply.

"Obviously not," I hear her murmur.

* * * *

Level two turns out to be the lowest level of a basement that looks like it might span the entire building. Nigel hands me a key and lifts his chin. "Down that hall. Number 6. He's waiting."

The floor is covered in stone, as are the walls. My boots click loudly as I make my way down the hall. I scan the information Eve provided on Louis, no last name listed. Profession: Self-Employed. I make note of his safe word, his list of no-goes. There are to be no marks on his body when he leaves. No cutting. No needles or hooks. Claustrophobic? No. What does he want? To be restrained, at my mercy. He sent some photos depicting mummification. Perfect.

I slide the skeleton key into the lock and then push open the door.

"About time!" Louis calls out. He's young, mid-twenties. Dressed in baggy jeans and a black T-shirt.

I drop my bag on the floor then stride over to him, swing my arm back, and slap his face, hard.

His eyes widen.

"You'll speak when spoken to. You'll get attention from me when I want to give it. Understand?"

"Yes."

"Yes, Domina!" I bark. "Say it."

"Yes, Domina," he repeats, lowering his head. His shoulder length dark hair falls in front of his green eyes. When I say nothing more, he glances up briefly. The eyes flick to the wolf, then back down again.

Even in the dim light of the dungeon, I recognize the young man. His poster is plastered on the walls of millions of teenaged girls worldwide. His concerts are sellouts. He has a clothing line and a new reality TV show. He's been in and out of rehab. Perhaps now he's looking for a new high.

"Strip. Do it quickly." I'm aware that the clock is ticking.

The lad pulls off his T-shirt in one fluid movement and tosses it onto the floor. The tennis shoes are kicked off. Boxers and jeans are pulled past his narrow hips without his having to pause to unzip or unbutton. He's left standing in his socks.

My riding crop cuts through the air with a high-pitched *whoosh* as it moves to point at his feet.

He scrabbles to remove the last remnants of clothing, hopping first on one foot, then the other to pull off his socks. His cock is partially erect. When I pull my handcuffs from my bag, it gets even more so. The dungeon is equipped with everything a Dominatrix could want or need. I make my way over to him, my riding crop poking the center of his chest. Pushing him back until he's just where I want him.

"On you knees. Lower your eyes. Hands out."

He obeys my commands. He's rock hard now. Within a matter of seconds I have him in cuffs. A chain attached to a pulley is looped through them. A few yanks, and Louis' body is stretched before me, arms held high above his head, toes just touching the floor.

"Suck me," he begs.

That earns him another slap. Clearly, he wasn't filled in on the rules. There's a roll of duct tape on a nearby table. I cut off a six-inch strip using a pair of surgical scissors and place it over his mouth. A second strip over his eyes.

"Come, and you will be punished," I hiss in his ear before picking up a large roll of plastic wrap. His body gets a quick dusting of power. I place some cotton padding between his ankles and knees. Then, I begin wrapping, circling around him from the legs up. He said on the form he wanted to be at my mercy, and I show him some—I leave his cock unbound and coax him to take a deep breath as I reach his chest.

Within six minutes, I'm close to finishing the job. Louis is covered in plastic wrap up to his collarbone. I lower his arms. His hands go to his cock. I don't bother to scold him. Instead I bind his arms in place just out of reach before grabbing the tilt table and securing him to it. It takes ten minutes for me to completely imprison him in plastic. He's immobile, safe.

"Come, and you will be punished," I remind him before slipping a cockring over the tip of his weeping penis. "Submit, and you will be rewarded."

While I've been busy, so has the wolf. But now his restless pacing has stopped. He eyes Louis warily. I check my watch, Torres should be with Eve now. I reach for the bag and head for the door. Cerberus covers the sounds of my leaving with a vigorous shake. With no time to spare I head away from the stairs and back to the elevator that the clients use. Since appointments are booked on the hour, it should be empty. And with the key Zack gave me, I can switch it into Firefighter service mode and go straight to Eve's apartment. No need for a special code. No need to pick any locks.

The elevator rises three floors above reception to open in a hallway. Eve's living quarters are spacious. Two bedrooms, two and a half baths, kitchen, dining room, living room, and office. I wouldn't say the space is lavishly decorated, but the furnishings are elegant, the overall décor tasteful. I swiftly move from room to room planting the devices as quickly as I can, aware that Louis is waiting, that Torres will only be able to hold Eve's attention for so long. In the corner of the living room is an old-fashioned roll top. It looks like it's used more for storage than a desk. It's piled with papers and books nearly to the top of the open tambour. I place the last bug there then race back to the elevator and down to the dungeon.

I take care in unwrapping Louis, carefully cutting through the plastic, covering his exposed skin with warm, wet towels that would slowly cool, drying his body with shearling mitts. The process keeps him on edge, my commands and the silicone band around his penis prevents him from going over. I taunt and tease, leaving him both satisfied and not.

"My reward?" he asks, hopefully.

The question earns him another slap.

He falls to his knees, lowers his head. "I can pay you."

"Pay me with your obedience. You're reward is that I'll agree to see you again."

"But—"

"Have I given you permission to speak further?"

"No, Domina," he replies, his voice strained from the effort to control himself.

Finally, I instruct him to go home, cockring in place. And to keep himself on the edge until the stroke of midnight.

* * * *

My second client is female and a fan of foot worship. An Assistant District Attorney who, under her cashmere overcoat is dressed like a French maid and content to spend the entirety of her session on her knees, bare ass in the air, licking my boots. While she makes satisfied noises Cerberus, restless, circles the room. After the DA experiences two spontaneous earthshaking orgasms she leaves me, with saliva all over my boots and a very agitated wolf.

With Cerberus glued to my side I retrace my previous steps in search of Nigel. I find him, flirting with the hostess.

I turn in the iPad

"Eve wants you to call her in the morning," he says handing me a wad of cash. "Louis is leaving the city to continue his tour and wants you to travel with him as part of his entourage."

I remember what Maitlan said about Eve: *There's nothing she can't arrange… for a price.*

"Lucky me."

Nigel frowns.

"I'll call first thing in the morning," I assure him before slipping out the side door into the darkness of the alley.

Cerberus surprises me by taking off at a dead run. I call out, but he doesn't stop. I can't keep up. I couldn't even if I'd been wearing sensible footwear. When I round the corner, there's no sign of the wolf. I whistle and listen, but all I hear are the sounds of the streets. I head back to the car, hoping that Cerberus will be there.

Instead I find Zack, naked and breathless behind the dumpster. He's in a crouched position, his back to me. I reach out and touch his shoulder.

"Are you all right?"

His body is slick with sweat and hot to the touch.

"Give me a minute, then toss me my clothes."

I leave him to catch his breath. Drop my bag into the back seat of the SUV and retrieve Zack's shirt and slacks. From experience I know not to bother searching for underwear. Clothes in hand, I head back.

"I need another minute," Zack calls out as I approach.

When I come around the side of dumpster, I see why. In the dim light I see the outline of his body. His hands are gripping the edge of the colossal metal container. In addition to his arms and legs, there's another appendage jutting out—fully erect.

"Oh!"

His head drops. "I've always been a fan of your work," he says, dryly. Then, "I need to burn this off. You take the car. I'll run back."

He extends his hand.

I take it.

I imagine confusion marring his brow as I place his clothes on top of the container and step closer to him. What he wants is his pants. What he needs is release. My tongue swipes across one erect nipple, the lick is slow and leisurely.

"What are you doing?"

I smile. "You know what I'm doing. Ask yourself if I'm enjoying it."

He wraps his hand in my hair. "I don't have to ask. I can smell your arousal," he replies, his voice rough with want. "I'm drowning in it, Emma. God help me, I want to drown in you." He lowers his head. His lips touch my ear. I feel his stubble against my cheek. "I'm still mad at you."

It's said in a whisper fit for the confessional.

"Good," I tell him, my hand circling his erection.

He unzips the catsuit, nuzzles the spot where he'd bitten me just days ago. The gesture reminds me that I'm walking a fine and dangerous line.

"You told me once that sex doesn't hold the same meaning for you that it does for me. That it doesn't hold any meaning for you," he says.

"That's right." I turn around, assuming the position he was in when I came upon him moments ago. Hands on the lid of the dumpster, legs spread apart.

His body is pressed against mine. His cock prodding my ass as he unzips my suit, slides his hands inside to cup my breasts.

I slip my arms out and push the leather down, exposing my torso, then my ass.

"Sometimes is doesn't hold any meaning for me either," he murmurs. "You sure you're okay with that?"

Ever the gentleman.

Zack's teasing my nipples, grinding against my ass. I'm dripping wet, on the verge of coming. I want him inside of me more than I want air. "Shut up and fuck me."

CHAPTER EIGHT

Hot water sluices down my back. My hair is washed, my face already scrubbed clean. As soon as we got back to the penthouse I headed for the shower, leaving Zack to update Torres and Maitlan. I turn off the taps, lean against the tiles of the back wall. They're cool and soothing. The last of the water circles the drain in a swirl. As I watch it go down, I remember a piece of advice my best friend Liz gave me when Zack first moved to San Diego.

Fool around all you want with Zack. Fuck him senseless every night. You've had hundreds of lovers. You just need to make sure he understands it's nothing serious. That it can't be anything serious. Keep your feelings hidden. The greatest sex he's ever had completely without strings? No man on earth would turn down a relationship like that.

Only I'd been convinced Zack would. That the feelings he held for me wouldn't allow him to enter into a relationship of convenience. Was I wrong?

I step out of the shower and towel off.

"So, you and Agent Monroe?"

It's Maitlan's voice on the other side of the door. He's in Zack's room.

"Are partners," Zack finishes.

I'm frozen in place.

"It's more than that. I noticed the way you didn't look at one another when you came back, lovers concealing an affair. Afraid to look at one another, that even a glance might reveal too much. Corrine and I were like that once. Until we just couldn't stand it anymore. Our fathers were business rivals. They hated one another. Never agreed on anything. Except that their grandson was perfect, of course."

"Of course," repeats Zack. Then, "I'm going to change, maybe go for a quick run."

"I'll leave you to it."

"Roger?"

"Hmm?"

"What you and Corrine had? That's not how it is with Emma and me. For a time I thought maybe... But I was wrong. It meant nothing to her. It was a thing. It was casual. It's over. End of story. Don't stir the pot. Okay?"

"Understood."

Silence filled the room.

It was a thing. It was casual. It's over. End of story.

He'd used those identical words to describe his relationship with Sarah at one point in time. A she-wolf he'd previously been involved with. I wait until he's changed his clothes and left the room. Then I tell myself this is exactly what I want. What Liz said Zack and I need. I should be relieved. I am relieved, relieved and sad. I let the sadness wash over me. Give myself a moment to wallow in it. Then push it aside, dry my hair and dress. Wearing a pair of sweats and a comfortable T-shirt, I head downstairs to do what I must.

Torres, O'Neill, and Bradley are wrapping up a call with the ATF when I enter the conference room.

"They find something?" I ask.

Bradley speaks up. "The trash can Maitlan was supposed to drop the money in had a hole in the bottom. It wasn't terribly damaged in the blast. They did a reconstruction."

"And it looks like it had been relocated a few feet so that it was right on top of a manhole cover," O'Neill adds.

I pour myself a cup of coffee and pull up a chair at the table. "So someone was waiting for the money in the sewer. What do we know about the bomb?"

Torres answers this one. "It was inside a nearby electrical box, made of C4. Looks like they used a wireless detonator. So, they had control over the timing. My guess is that the plan was to blow it after the drop to create a distraction—"

"Or to kill Maitlan after fucking with him for hours," I interject.

Torres continues, "But Maitlan made Devlin in the café, and she had to act."

"If something went wrong, it stands to reason she'll reach out to her accomplices. Right?" asks O'Neill.

"Listen up!" Bradley sits up straight in his chair. "Someone's entered Devlin's apartment."

Bradley flips a switch and we can suddenly hear heels clacking against a polished wooden floor. I pick up my phone to text Zack, but he sweeps into the conference room before I have a chance to start dialing. He's fresh from a shower, dressed in jeans and a sweatshirt, hair still wet and combed straight back.

"She's in the apartment. Or, someone is. A woman," I tell him.

Eve's voice fills the room. "It's me. The FBI was here today, asking questions."

"What kinds of questions?" asks a male voice.

"She's has the guy on speaker. Let me grab Maitlan. See if he recognizes the voice," Zack says.

"They said it was routine," Eve replies.

There's a long pause.

Just as the man begins to speak again, Zack returns with Maitlan.

"What the fuck happened? The bomb wasn't supposed to be detonated until after the drop. Burt was in the sewer, ready to catch the backpack when all hell broke loose."

"I *told* you!" Maitlan's voice is ragged with anger. "You can arrest her now. Make her talk. Right?"

Zack holds up his hand, demanding silence.

"He was walking away. He wasn't going to pay. It's time to end this," says Eve, her tone commanding.

"What does she mean?" Maitlan's voice has dropped to a whisper. He begins pacing. One hand clenching his stomach, the other rising to cover his mouth.

"We haven't gotten our money," says the man.

"I'll get you the money as soon as you finish the

job. Kill the boy. Tomorrow morning we bury him."

"No!" Maitlan grasps the front of Zack's shirt. "Zack, no!"

"We?" The male voice asks.

"I want to see the body. Make sure you have the balls to do what needs to be done."

"Oh, we've got the balls," he assures her.

Maitlan is crumbling. "Can't you trace the call?"

I shake my head. "She's not using her landline or her cell. She must be using a burner."

"There's got to be something you can—"

The rest of his sentence is swallowed up by the sound of a gunshot.

Every one of us is frozen in place, frozen in time.

We failed.

My eyes meet Zack's.

He's trying to support Maitlan, but it's no use. The man has fallen to his knees.

Everyone in the room is silent, except for Zack. He's on the floor with his friend, cradling him as he would a child, whispering words meant to comfort. Only none of us can hear them over the soul-wrenching wails of a grieving father.

In all my years as an FBI agent, I've never experienced anything like this. Oh, I've lost kidnap victims—it's a sad reality of this job. But to hear one being killed while we listen helpless is something new and inconceivably horrible.

I feel like *I've* taken a shot in the gut. Bile rushes up, burning the back of my throat. An ice-cold chill brushes the back of my neck. My hands are balled up into tight fists, and I realize my nails are digging into my palms. The pain brings me back. I swallow, stiffen my spine, and move to help support my partner, to help console Maitlan.

By the time I reach them, Maitlan's pushed Zack away and he's climbed to his feet. The man is wide-eyed, tugging at his hair, pacing back and forth like a caged animal. "You promised me you'd get him back!" he spits the words at Zack, who stands there and takes it.

"I'm sorry, Roger," he says, his own voice cracking.

But Maitlan is inconsolable and angry and looking for someone to unload on. He rushes Zack, fists flying. Zack allows Maitlan to get in one good shot across his jaw before wrapping the man in a tight embrace.

Bradley and I move toward them, but Zack holds up a hand telling us to back off. Maitlan is crumbling once again.

"I'm going to take him upstairs." Zack says the words softly.

I nod. Torres is standing beside me. "I'm so sorry," she says.

Maitlan's face is buried in his hands. He neither looks up nor responds to her words. Zack leads him out of the room, an arm around his shoulders.

As soon as Maitlan and Zack are out of earshot, Torres rounds on me. "We fucked up," she says. "We should have grabbed Eve. Interrogated the shit out of her. Made her tell us where she stashed Robby."

The same combination of anger and guilt seethes inside me. If we'd had Eve, I could have gotten the truth out of her. We thought we had more time. We thought we understood her motivations. We were wrong.

"We can get her with this," I say, pointing to the receiver. "She's on the record telling them to kill the boy. Not much comfort to Maitlan, but at least he'll know she's going to be punished. I know it might feel counter-intuitive. But this isn't the time to bring her in. The worst has already happened. We have an opportunity here. We need to use Eve to get to her accomplices."

Torres turns to O'Neill. "Whatever surveillance we have on her now, double it. We need our best on this detail. They need to be ghosts."

O'Neill nods, start's dialing.

"So we watch and wait?" asks Bradley. "We wait for her to go meet them?" He's furiously typing on his keyboard. She owns a car, one of the new BMW SUV's." He smiles. "It has Intelligent Emergency Call and Connected Drive Services. We can override it so even if she turns it off we'll be able to track her."

"Get whatever we're going to need in place. Check credit card statements. See if she uses a car or taxi service. We want to be ready to intercept any calls and cover all possibilities. We'll listen, we'll watch. And in the morning we'll follow her." Torres turns to me, "You're dead on your feet. So is your partner. We're going to need you both functioning by dawn. Get a few hours of rest. We can handle this."

She's right, I know. Torres and her team are competent, more than competent. I stand up, stretch, and release a breath. "I'll check on Maitlan and Zack, then try to get some sleep. Wake me if there's a development?"

"Of course."

I leave them and begin to climb the long staircase that leads to Maitlan's living quarters. My body is heavy with fatigue and remorse. My bones ache. I have to lay down, but I fear I won't get any sleep, We simply can't fail tomorrow. I didn't say it to Torres, but in addition to nailing Eve's ass to the wall and capturing her co-conspirators, getting Robby's body back is a priority. I've seen what happens to parents who are never able to lay their children to rest. It adds another layer of pain to an already unbearable situation. I won't let Maitlan go thorough that agony, too.

In the distance, I hear the ringing of a phone.

"Wait, Emma!"

I'm already racing back down the stairs and into the conference room. Torres has her headset on. The call is coming in on the ransom line. She nods at me. I pick up the receiver and hold it to my ear.

"Yes?"

"Let me speak to Maitlan." It's a male voice, distorted. A recognizable voice.

The same voice that we recorded on earlier ransom calls.

What kind of game is this guy playing? "He's not here at the moment."

"Well, get him. If he wants to see his kid alive again, he'd better talk to me. Now."

My heart is hammering against my ribs. I can't let on that we overheard Eve order them to kill Robby, or that we heard the sound of a gunshot in response to that order.

Could it be that was for Eve's benefit? Are they working on their own now?

My eyes lock with Torres'. "He'll want to speak with the boy," I say. "After what happened this afternoon, we're going to need proof of life."

"What happened this afternoon wasn't our fault. We were prepared to make the exchange. Maitlan can speak to Robby. Now, you have two minutes to get him on the line."

O'Neill has already fled the room, calling out for Maitlan and Zack. I silently count down the seconds. Will Maitlan refuse to come down? Will he think it's a cruel joke?

No. Like a drowning man, he's desperate to grab onto anything that will buoy him, give him hope. He's back downstairs in less than ninety seconds, Zack close on his heels.

"This is real?" he asks.

The line is on hold. "We think so. Remember, we did not hear Eve order Robby's death. We did not hear that gun shot. All we know is that there was a fucked up drop. Maybe the bomb was unrelated. You did what you were supposed to do. You want your son back. You have the money."

He snatches the phone from my hand. "I got it. I got it."

Bradley presses a button and the call connects.

"This is Maitlan. Let me talk with Robby."

A moment's silence on the line. Then a tremorous voice fills the room. "Daddy?"

Maitlan's knees sag. He drops into a chair. "Is that really you, son?"

"I'm scared and—"

The remainder of the boy's sentence is muffled. We hear the sound of a door close.

"I need to hear that he's all right. Unharmed. Put my son back on the damn phone!" he demands.

"You heard his voice. You know he's alive. Now we talk about the money."

"The money. I was ready to pay the ransom this afternoon. Someone might get the impression you guys didn't really want it."

"You've got it wrong. The money is all we want. We were as surprised as you. We were there, ready to make the exchange. We're ready to go ahead now. But the price has gone up. We want twenty million. Get it. We'll call back at three this afternoon with instructions. And Maitlan, we know the FBI is involved. But if you try to fuck us, you'll never see your kid again. This is your last chance. You come alone to the drop, and we all part friends. Got it?"

"Yes, I've got it. Twenty million. You'll call at three. Can I please speak—" The call is killed.

Maitlan spins around in his chair to face Zack. "He's not dead," he whispers. "He's not dead."

"But Eve thinks he is," I remind him. "First she double-crosses them with the ransom drop."

"Now it looks as if they're double-crossing her," Zack adds.

Torres removes her headset and tosses it onto the table. "This is the break we've been waiting for. We'll follow Eve tomorrow. She'll lead us to the kidnappers and Robby."

Zack leans back against the doorjamb. "She'll lead us somewhere," he says. "But my guess is that the kidnappers and Robby will be long gone."

But Torres remains hopeful. "Unless they're looking for revenge. Could be they are planning a burial. Just not Robby's."

"Best case scenario, we nab them all and bring Robby home safe and sound," I say. "If they've already cleared out, we'll at least have Eve leading us to the scene where Robby was held. We can make her give up her accomplices. Once she realizes they've thrown her under the bus, that shouldn't be hard."

"And, we have a pretty persuasive bargaining chip. The tape of her telling them to kill Robby," adds O'Neill. "She'll have a tough time denying involvement. She's a smart woman. She'll know she's looking at hard time. Eve's going to want to deal."

And if she doesn't, I think, I'll leave her no choice, use my own method of bargaining.

Maitlan looks like a condemned man minutes away from execution who has been granted an unexpected full pardon. He's now standing strong, shoulders back, hands steady. "I'll phone my friend at the bank and tell him to get the money ready."

But his eyes are still shadowed and dull. His face worn from stress and worry. Zack reaches out and gives Maitlan's shoulder a squeeze. "Then try to get some sleep. We have a long day ahead of us tomorrow. You're going to need to be strong for your son when we get him back."

Maitlan gives us a weary smile. "I'm sorry for…" He points to Zack's jaw.

Zack shrugs. "You needed to hit something. Glad I could be of service. Now, go make that call."

"If you don't mind," Torres interjects, "when

you're done, we'll trade off catching a couple hours each on the sofa in your office. It's going to be a long day for all of us."

"Not a problem. There's a shower across the hall if you need it. It connects to both the office and the gym. It'll be yours in five minutes."

Once he's gone. O'Neill stands up and stretches. "I could use a workout and a shower. Give me an hour, then I can hold down the post while you two catch some Z's."

Bradley waves him off. "Knock yourself out." He turns to Torres. "I'll take first shift. No sense you waiting up with me. If anything happens, you'll be right across the hall. I expect we have at least until daybreak. Eve believes her orders were carried out. She thinks the boy is already dead."

So much has happened in the last few hours, I feel whip-lashed. Sex with Zack outside Elysium; hearing Eve order Robby's death; the sound of the gunshot; the unexpected bombshell that Robby is still alive. I'm numb from the shock of it all. I can't even imagine how Maitlan is feeling.

Zack startles me by placing a hand on my arm. "You okay?"

I look into his face. I wonder if I should tell him that I heard what he said to Maitlan about us—that we had a thing, that it was casual and over, end of story.

Hardly seems worth the effort. I shrug. "Yes."

He cocks his head, looks at me. Waits.

"No," I admit. "When the call came in, I was heading upstairs. What you said to Maitlan is true for us too. We need to at least get a couple hours of rest."

"I'm going to check on Roger, then I'll be right behind you."

* * * *

Back in my assigned room, I don't bother undressing or changing. I just slip out of my shoes, push the array of decorative pillows off of the queen-sized bed, then flop down face first. I don't even pull down the covers. Images and sounds flit through my mind, but I can't hold on to a single one. I feel like I'm flying, weightless, defying the laws of gravity like I used to. Then falling plummeting toward a place called Elysium.

There's a knock.

I lift my head and look back. Through bleary eyes I see Zack, backlit by the bathroom light. He's standing just inside my room, holding a roll of what appears to be duck tape.

"I have something for you," he says.

I let my head fall back down onto the pillow. "Something no Siren in her right mind would turn down." Laughter bubbles up out of me. Did I say that out loud?

I feel the bed shift, the lamp on the bedside table snaps on.

Zack places his thumb under my eye and gently pulls it down to examine the inside of my lower lid. "You're anemic. Kallistos' text said you might need more blood, so I've been keeping a close eye on you." he says. "Though I loathe to admit it, he was right."

If I'd been able to sleep, to eat properly, to stay

hydrated, Kallistos' infusing me with his blood would have been enough to heal me, more than enough. But I haven't. I've been running myself ragged. I hear the screech of tape being stripped from the roll. I turn over, blinking against the brightness. Zack is taping something to the bedpost. "Where did you get blood?"

"Does it matter? It's safe. You need it." Zack straightens my arm, rubs a spot in the crease of my elbow with alcohol, then places a tourniquet around by bicep.

"But you don't know my blood type. I don't like needles."

"I don't need to. This is type O. Close your eyes." I feel a prick as the needle breaks the skin then nothing as he releases the tourniquet and then uses surgical tape to secure the line so it and the needle won't move.

I open one eye and glance down. The tube connecting the bag to the needle in my arm is now running red. "You're pretty good at that."

"I've had some experience. This is going to take three or four hours to run." He reaches for the riding crop that I'd carelessly thrown on the bed and neglected to remove. "We'll use this as a splint. It will help prevent you from bending or moving your arm." More surgical tape is wound around my arm.

I place my hand over his. "It is vampire blood?"

Zack sighs. He pulls the sweatshirt he's wearing over his head and extends his bandage-covered arm. "It's my blood. Let's get you under the covers."

He pulls them back and I awkwardly slide in.

Zack turns off the light then moves around to the

other side of the bed. "I'm staying with you. If you notice anything off, fever, chills, headache, nausea. Wake me."

Before I have a chance to register any protest, he's managed to turn me on my side and curl himself around me.

"I'm sorry, Emma." I feel the beat of his breath against the back of my hair.

"For what?"

There's a long pause. "I wish I knew. For the secrets between us, I guess. For the lies. For our inability to be honest with one another."

Cocooned in the darkness with Zack's body wrapped around mine, I asked the question that had been nagging at me. "Were you being truthful when you said you loved me? Or when you told Maitlan that what we had was casual. Over." Sleep was tugging mercilessly at my consciousness.

"At the time the declaration was heartfelt and true," he says.

Was.

"I'd trust you with my life, Emma."

Tears leak out of the corners of my eyes. I nod and try not to sound as sad and angry as I feel. I've been here before with another man, a man I thought I could love and protect. Lesson learned. I reach for Zack's hand and place it over my breast. I take a few quiet breaths to steady myself. To tamp down the emotion that wants to cling to my voice. Then I say what I must.

"Just don't ever, ever, trust me with your heart."

CHAPTER NINE

Day Three: Monday, September 9

By six we're all sitting around the conference room table. Maitlan has supplied us with bagels and cream cheese, coffee and juice. We're refreshed, refueled, and ready. Now it's time for the waiting game. A few minutes after six thirty, Eve places a call, again using the speaker function.

The call goes immediately to voicemail. There's no greeting. My guess is the guys have dumped it. We hear a growl of frustration followed by a crash. The line disconnects.

"Somebody's not having a good morning," says Torres, smiling into her cup of Joe.

There's a flurry of activity in Eve's apartment. She picks up her landline and calls down to the concierge, ordering that her car be brought around. Footfalls on the hardwood floors allow me to imagine her moving around her apartment. Finally there's the *bing* of an elevator. She's heading to the garage. My guess, to her SUV.

I look up at Bradley. "You're all set to track her?"

"Piece of cake," he says.

Torres' cell phone buzzes. She listens for but a moment before disconnecting. "One of my guys confirmed Eve just left Elysium. She's in a white BMW SUV. They'll tail her at a safe distance until we can catch up."

Zack tosses his half-eaten bagel into the trash. "Bradley, you stay behind and handle coms. O'Neill, Torres, Monroe, we'll head out in two separate cars."

"What about me? I'm going with you," says Maitlan.

Zack flashes him a look that says he'll tolerate no arguments. "No. You're staying here. If the kidnappers get nervous and step up their timeline, we need to be ready. You need to be here. And you have to maintain a cool head. Remember, ask to speak to Robby. Agree to their demands. Bradley will talk you through it."

Maitlan nods. He looks at Bradley, his new lifeline. Then back at us. "I have a beater Chevy truck in the garage. Space 104. I barely drive the thing, I certainly don't take it to social events or Elysium. Eve wouldn't recognize it. The keys are marked and hanging by the elevator on the key rack."

"When will the money be here and ready?" asks Zack.

Maitlan checks his watch. "I called my banker last night. It's too much for me to waltz out of the bank with. They own an armored Mercedes. He's bagging up the money, placing the duffels in the trunk and driving it over. I should have it in hand by ten."

Zack turns to Bradley. "Keep a security detail on it."

"Will do."

"Roger?" Zack's hand is on Maitlan's arm. "You going to be all right?"

He narrows his eyes. "I will be as soon as I have my son back. Zack? Don't let them get away."

Zack releases his grip. "We won't."

* * * *

We pick up Eve's tail on I-87 N out of the city. Zack is riding shotgun. The two of us are in the lead car, our dress casual. Just two folks heading out of the city to enjoy a little fresh air for the day. Torres and O'Neill are following in a black sedan with tinted windows. Thanks to Bradley, we're all in communication.

"Where do you think she's heading?" Zack asks after we've been traveling thirty minutes.

"No cement, no skyscrapers. I think they call this the country," Torres replies dryly.

No kidding. We're surrounded by gently sloping farmland and green pastures. "It's hard to believe this is right outside New York City," I say.

"For how long, who knows?" Torres replies. "More and more families are selling out to developers. A few have preserved their farms, but the money is a great temptation to most."

"Does Eve have property out here?" I ask.

Bradley chimes in. "Not that I've been able to find."

We're a good ten car lengths behind Eve. An

impatient driver passes Torres, then us. He rolls down his window and flicks out a cigarette. I get the feeling he's about to pass Eve as we approach the turnoff to Underhill Avenue from the Taconic State Parkway, but he doesn't have to. Her turn signal flashes on.

"Here we go. She's turning," Zack says.

No sooner does she complete the turn, the guy ahead of us in the pick-up pulls off to the side of the road. "What an asshole." I mutter. "He passes us just to pull over?"

"He's one of ours," replies Torres. "We're trying to create the illusion of additional traffic. Makes us less conspicuous."

We continue to follow Eve from a safe distance. A range rover marked as a Sheriff's car drives past us on the opposite side of Underhill Ave. "He one of ours too?" Zack asks.

"No sir," Torres confirms. "He's out here all on his own."

If the sudden appearance of the Sheriff made Eve nervous, it's not evident. And there's no sign that she's aware of being followed.

"It looks like she's going to turn on Baptist Church Road," I announce. "Do I follow?"

I can hear Bradley clicking away on his keyboard. "There's a popular farm store out that way," he says. "But it's on a two-lane road and not open for the day yet, so it's too early for there to be much traffic. I can re-route Torres once we know where Eve's headed. Emma, you go ahead and take the turn. Aside the store, there are only a couple farms out that way. If she turns on Croton, you keep going on Baptist Church Road. Pull over and wait. As soon as Eve reaches her destination, I'll let you know. We're close, I can feel it."

Bradley's hunch is correct. Eve makes another right onto Croton Avenue. I drive past the turn off, then pull over. The road we're on now is narrow, framed on both sides by thick woods. Two additional SUV's come out of nowhere.

"I thought we couldn't trust anyone?" Torres asks.

"These guys aren't local. They're with the Hostage Rescue Team." Zack turns to me and adds, "Jastremski and some of his boys. You'll remember him from Charleston."

Torres' vehicle stops just behind them. She and O'Neill spill out of their sedan. Eight other agents, dressed in flak jackets and weapons drawn, emerge from the SUV's. Zack and Jastremski don't bother with introductions.

"We're at your disposal," Jastremski says, grasping Zack's hand.

"Appreciate you coming," Then to us he says, "Everyone suit up."

I put on my vest and tighten the straps. Suddenly I'm missing the custom one Zack had made for me. Not only was it lighter weight, it provided me with better coverage.

"She's stopped," says Bradley. "The car pulled into a long dirt driveway that's opposite the thicket of trees you're in front of. The tree line curves around to the back of the property. You could approach from there pretty easily."

"Send me a satellite image," Zack orders.

"Sure thing."

Within seconds Zack is studying the photo on his phone. "It looks like a small cabin."

"Are there any other cars in the area?" Torres asks.

Bradley answers. "No." I've been scanning the surrounding woods. "I'm not seeing any other nearby activity.

Zack pulls his personal vest from a duffel and slips it on. I have a hunch he's wishing Betsy was in there too. "Any of your guys have an extra sniper rifle?"

Jastremski points to one of his men. "Hansen will set you up." Zack tosses the duffel in my direction before going to seek out the agent. "You're going to want this."

I look inside.

My vest.

He packed it.

It takes me seconds to change. By that time Zack's returned.

We all gather around.

"We'll use the trees for cover," Zack says. "Once we reach this clearing we surround the place. There's a door in back and one in front. We're not taking any chances. Jastremski, take three of your men and cover the sides of the house. Send two with Emma and me. My team will take the front."

Hanson and a third guy joins Zack and me.

Jastremski picks three of his remaining five for his team. "These last two?"

"With Torres and O'Neill. Torres' team will go in through the back. We move fast, stay in communication, and coordinate. Got it?"

Heads bob up and down.

Bradley's voice cuts in, "I just heard from Quantico, the Forensics team they're sending is an hour out."

Torres has already slipped her gun from the holster at the small of her back. "So we secure the cabin and then do our best to leave it undisturbed. Everyone remember, this is very likely a crime scene. We don't want to contaminate any evidence."

It's not difficult going, so we're able to move with swift precision. The low-growing brush and the trees are spaced close enough to conceal us. The moist, flat ground is covered with a cushion of pine needles and dropped leaves that mask the sounds of our approach. We leave Torres, O'Neill and two other men at the rear of the house. Jastremski sends two others to cover the east side. Then Zack and I move with him and the remaining toward the west, guns drawn. Jastremski's team stays behind to monitor from that vantage point, the remaining continue on with us. We circle around to the front. The only car in the driveway is Eve's. The house is small. There are three steps leading up to a modest porch. Large windows are covered with heavy curtains drawn. But the front door is open. Zack motions toward it with his gun.

My gut tells me the kidnappers are gone—and so is Robby. The two men accompanying us glide soundlessly onto the porch and position themselves, back flush against the outside of the house.

The air is still.

My heart is pounding.

"Son of a bitch," Eve shrieks. The oath is

accompanied by the sound of breaking glass as something is thrown against the wall.

"We're going in," Zack tells the others.

One of the guys reaches for the handle to the screen door and swings it wide open. Zack is the first to go through, rifle across his back, Glock leading the way.

I enter in time to see him level it at Eve's chest.

"On the floor," he says. "It's over."

* * * *

The remainder of the small, two-bedroom farmhouse is quickly cleared. The place was cleaned, surfaces wiped, but in a hurry. The smell of bleach clings to the air. The trashcans outside are empty. Torres and O'Neill are busy with the forensics team. A small pile of cigarettes smoked down to the nubs was found on the ground just off the porch. One beer bottle was missed that had rolled under the couch. The windows in the bedroom and the top of the sash had no prints, but there was a partial thumbprint under the sash. They also scored with the metal roller inside the toilet paper holder. Most damning was a child's pajama top. It was found between the mattress and the wall, perhaps when the twin bed was stripped of its sheets. One surreptitious sniff told Zack it was Robby's. The boy had been here. For the benefit of everyone else, he then made a call to Maitlan and sent him a picture of the cotton T-shirt with the Superman insignia on it. Maitlan confirmed the top matched the one Robby had on when he was taken.

We have Eve. She's sitting rather uncomfortably in the back of one of the SUV's. Mirandized and manacled in my handcuffs. She can hear bits and pieces of conversation among the team as they drift in and out of the house.

"It's just a matter of time before we identify your accomplices," says Zack. "Once we do, you'll have nothing to bargain with. Nothing we need. And, frankly, I like that idea. Let's just all continue to sit here and enjoy the fresh air."

"Accomplices," she mutters. "I don't know what you're talking about. This cabin belongs to a friend of mine. I come up here to get away from the city."

"Right. Cause you're a country girl at heart," I say.

She narrows her eyes and peers at me. "I know you, don't I?"

I shake my head. "Doubt it."

Zack suppresses a grin. Without make-up and dressed in jeans and a blazer over a shirt that looks as if I slept in it (which I did), this plain-jane FBI agent could never be confused for a dominatrix—especially one who made her entrance with a wolf on a lead.

I pick up where my partner left off. "You sure you don't want to come clean with us, Eve? Kidnapping is a serious crime. If Robby is still alive, you may not spend the rest of your life in prison. If he isn't, and you could have helped us, you'll have seen Elysium for the last time. And, let's face it. A gal like you isn't going to have an easy time of it in prison."

She turns her head away. It tells me we're making progress.

"It's up to you," adds Zack.

"I told you, I don't know what you're talking about." Her attention is drawn by the sound of Torres' footfalls on the wooden porch. She looks over at Torres. "I told that cop last night. I haven't seen Maitlan for weeks and I've never seen his son. You can't prove otherwise."

I'm tiring of this cat and mouse game. I know I can get Eve to speak the truth. All it would take would be a few seconds of my own special brand of interrogation, but maybe we don't need that, not with the recorded evidence Zack has in his pocket. Right on cue he pulls it out and turns it on. When Eve's hears her own voice, her eyes widen in shock.

"It's me. The FBI was here today, asking questions."

"What kinds of questions?" asks a male voice.

"They said it was routine," Eve replies.

"What the fuck happened? The bomb wasn't supposed to be detonated until after the drop. Burt was in the sewer, ready to catch the backpack when all hell broke loose."

"He was walking away. He wasn't going to pay. It's time to end this," says Eve, her tone commanding.

"We haven't gotten our money," says the man.

"I'll get you the money as soon as you finish the job. Kill the boy. Tomorrow morning we bury him."

"We?" The male voice asks.

"I want to see the body. Make sure you have the balls to do what needs to be done."

"Oh, we've got the balls," he assures her.

A gunshot blasts over the line.

Zack clicks off the recorder. "Still want to tell us

you don't know what we're talking about?"

Eve starts to shake and stammer, the cool façade begins to fade away. "How did you get that?"

"We've been on to you for a while," I snap. "And we can put you away for a long time with what's on that tape. Conspiracy to commit murder, for starters. You may not have pulled the trigger, but you ordered the kill."

Zack continues, "In fact, you might be surprised to learn that no one has pulled a trigger... yet."

"Your pals double-crossed you, Eve," I tell her, flashing her a confident smile. "They contacted us yesterday to demand ransom. They've cut you loose. You have one chance to help us, and the clock is ticking."

Eve is quiet—the battle raging in her head reflected on her face.

Torres calls out to us. "Found a toothpick that was concealed by the seat cushion of a chair."

"Fucking Burt," spits Eve.

"Burt, who?" I press.

She turns to us, eyes wide, projecting vulnerability. As if either Zack or I would ever forget Eve's the one who set all of this in motion. "You have to protect me." It comes out in a rush.

"Protect you from whom?" I ask, struggling to keep the edge out of my voice.

Eve draws a deep breath and closes her eyes. "From the police."

"The police?" Zack asks.

"The men who have Robby. They're cops."

By now Torres has joined us. "What the fuck are you talking about?" Torres steps closer, eyes blazing. "I don't believe her. We don't need to deal. We have prints and DNA."

Eve looks at her from beneath lowered brows. "But that will take time, won't it? And little Robby might not have much." She meets Torres' gaze. "You'd be amazed how many of you blue bloods belong to Elysium. And not only cops, judges, district attorneys, city officials. We offer certain discrete services they can't find any where else."

"Not interested in your clientele," I break in. "Or your services. Who has Robby?"

"If I tell you, what will you do for me?"

Torres snaps. I have to grab her arm to keep her from lunging at Eve.

"Who has Robby?" I repeat, forcing calm into my voice. "Tell us. Now."

"And you'll tell the D.A. I cooperated?"

"Yes," Zack replies:

"I'll want that in writing," she says.

Next thing you know, she's going to be calling for her lawyer. We don't have time for this. I turn to Torres. "Walk it off. Give us five."

As soon as she's gone, I lean into the car and unleash my rage. I don't bother with finesse or control. I let the magic break through. A gust of wind rips through the car.

"Bradley, can you record this?"

"Roger that," he replies.

I don't have to turn around to know Zack's retreated. This time, he's wisely made a run for it. I can see him through the car's rear window. He's sitting on the front stoop of the house, looking as if he's been punched in the gut.

"You okay?" One of the lab boys stops to check on him.

Zack nods.

I turn my attention back toward Eve who looks shaken and more than a little windblown. "Tell us what you know about the kidnapping of Robby Maitlan."

This time I say it with calm confidence. I know she's going to cooperate, that the information will be forthcoming. I had no choice. Now, neither does Eve.

CHAPTER TEN

"This is Special Agent Emma Monroe," I begin. Don't want to fuck this up by doing something that a good a defense lawyer could get tossed out. "I'm interviewing Eve Devlin in connection with the kidnapping of Robby Maitlan. This interview is being recorded. She has waived right to counsel and agrees to questioning. Right, Ms. Devlin?"

I see it in her eyes—the sense of simultaneous wonder and confusion. She can't look away from me. Numbly, she nods.

"You need to say it out loud," I prod. "Please repeat that you've waived your right to counsel for the recording."

"I've waived my right to counsel."

"Ms. Devlin, who has Robby?"

"Detectives Chuck Imperiale and Burt Benson. They're OCCB cops," she says.

"They're with Organized Crime Control?" I ask. "Why are they involved?"

"Why do you think?" She snaps back. "Money. This was to be a big payout for them, the one they've been waiting for." The words fall from her mouth like coins from a slot machine. She draws a breath and continues. "They've been taking bribes from me for years to ensure I keep my licenses and avoid any unwanted attention. They've been loyal lapdogs, *protecting* the anonymity of my clients. This was the score Imperiale's been waiting for, big enough for he and Benson to retire on. I promised them that with Maitlan's money, they could wave goodbye to the force, leave this cement jungle and move on to another place, another life."

"But then you double-crossed them. Why?"

"Because for me, it never was about the money." Her eyes are hard now, her words fired in staccato bursts. "Maitlan killed my daughter. I intended to return the favor. Take his son from him the way he took my daughter. I don't give a flying fig about Chuck and Burt."

"Before we started taping, you said you were afraid of them. You asked for protection," I remind her. I wait a beat and then make what sounds like an observation. "But you don't seem afraid of them now. We need to know the truth. Who's had the upper hand here? Were you coerced? Are you in need of protection, Ms. Devlin?"

"Coerced?" Eve snorts, "This was my idea, from start to finish. Those idiots have been eating out of the palm of my hand. What were they going to do? Arrest me? Turn me in? They couldn't very well do that without implicating themselves, could they? Especially not after they killed the babysitter. They're looking at life and I reminded them of that. They know what happens to cops in prison. As soon as Chuck killed that girl, they were mine."

Eve's satisfied smile gives me a chill. Was that

part of her master plan. Did she send them into Maitlan's home hoping for a casualty? Probably. I resist the temptation to speculate out loud about how a pretentious middle-aged madam might fare in prison. Instead I say, "But then they turned the tables on you. How did you lose control, Eve?"

"Incompetent bastards," Eve spits. "I should have known Burt wouldn't have the stomach to kill a kid. And Chuck? All he cared about was the money. My mother always said, you want something done right... I should have driven over here last night and killed the kid myself."

"I want to remind you, Ms. Devlin, you've waived your right to have an attorney present during questioning. This conversation is being recorded. Anything you say will be used against you. You did say you understood your rights."

Eve lapses into silence. I can tell she's struggling. She's answering because she has no choice, because the magic is making it impossible for her to resist. She knows she's hanging herself. I can see it in her eyes, she's struggling to reconcile what's happening and can't.

"Again, the recording won't register your nod. I need for you to say out loud that you understand."

"I understand," Eve admits through gritted teeth.

"One more question. Is anyone else aware of or involved in this?"

"No. No one else."

"Stop the recording, Bradley. We're finished." I remove my earpiece, hold it in the palm of my hand, then lean in close and whisper into Eve's ear. "You don't understand why you're cooperating. I'll tell you why. Because you're hoping it will encourage leniency and because of something else you remember your mother saying: Confession is good for the soul."

I've gotten what we needed. Before she has a chance to say anything further, I rein in my powers, slam the door shut, then smooth down my hair. Do I feel bad that I just manipulated Eve Devlin into a confession that's likely to put her away for the rest of her life? No. Not one bit.

I reinsert the earpiece and head over to meet Zack.

"Brilliant interrogation! You know it's..." he hesitates, searching for the right word. He lowers his voice a notch. "It's always a pleasure watching you work." The admiration in his voice rings true, but there's a hint of something else conveyed in his tone, in the way he's looking at me. Understanding.

I can already hear Agent Bradley tapping away on his keyboard. "OCCB officers Chuck Imperiale and Burt Benson have been partners for close to two years," he says. "While you were interrogating Devlin I called dispatch pretending to be one of Imperiale's CI's. They're both supposedly on vacation this week."

"Some vacation," Zack says. "How quickly can you get their home addresses?"

The words are no sooner out of his mouth. Our cell phones both buzz.

"Just sent them via text."

I catch Torres' eye and wave her over.

"Gotta hand it to you," she says. "For getting

the confession *and* for keeping you're cool."

Zack holds up his cell. "We've got addresses for Imperiale and Benson."

Torres nods. "I'll take care of getting Eve processed. You two should head back to the city with O'Neill, find out all you can about these two."

"Will you be taking the Hostage Rescue Team with you?" asks Bradley.

Zack doesn't hesitate. "No, we'll keep this low profile for now. We don't want to spook them. These guys are cops, they'll be monitoring police scanners and the local news. HRT will stay here until forensics arrives."

"I'll go tell O'Neill." Torres glances at her watch. "We still have four hours before the ransom call comes in. Do you think we'll be able to get to Imperiale and Benson first?"

"That's what I'm counting on." Zack says. He places his hand at the small of my back and steers me toward the pick up. "I'll drive, you navigate."

"Wait!" Torres holds out her car keys. "The sedan has GPS. You can plug in the addresses. "

Zack and Torres make a quick exchange of keys. She lets her voice drop. "Do you think we can trust Devlin? Do you really believe we're looking for two cops?"

Zack's eyes meet mine. He's told me on more than one occasion that I'm the only lie detector he's never been able to best.

"There's no doubt in my mind," he tells her.

We slide into the sedan and buckle up. O'Neill joins us.

"Hit the lights and hold on," Zack tells me before

putting the sedan in gear and stepping on the gas. Then to Bradley, "Do either of these guys live alone?"

It takes a couple minutes for an answer to come back. "Benson is thirty, married and has a Sunnyside address. The guys had two accommodations for Meritorious Police Duty—both for Community Service. Doesn't seem like the kind of guy who'd be mixed up in something like this. From the looks of his Facebook page, his wife is pregnant and he has two other kids. The oldest, Joey, is five. Madeline is three."

"What about his financials?" Zack asks.

The question is met with silence.

"What is it?" asks O'Neill.

"The kid, Joey, has cancer. Looks like it's gotten to the point that conventional treatment just isn't working anymore. Benson took him down to Mexico a couple weeks ago. There's a $30,000 charge from a clinic in Tijuana. They flew from La Guardia to San Diego on Southwest and then rented a car to go across the boarder."

"Could be what triggered this, the potential loss of his firstborn," I say.

Zack nods. "Alternative treatments are expensive and the insurance probably won't cover it. What about Imperiale?"

Bradley continues, "Imperiale is almost twenty years older. He lives in the Murray Hill area and is long divorced. His ex-wife got custody of the two kids. He's been paying child support for ages. Both of his girls are in college. He lives alone. And he's got a gambling problem. A big gambling problem. I'm seeing lots of weekend trips to Atlantic City.

Withdrawals from ATM's inside casinos. There's only a few hundred in his checking account, nothing left in savings. He's drained his 401K."

"Could be he sees this as a sure bet and an easy payday," O'Neill says.

"Could be he owes the wrong people," Zack suggests. "Bradley, keep digging. I want everything you can find on these two."

"I vote we go to Imperiale's first," O'Neill says. "Seems unlikely Benson would stash a kid in his house along with a pregnant wife."

"Agreed," Zack replies.

"There'll be a warrant waiting for you when you get there," Bradley chimes in.

"How's Maitlan holding up," I ask.

"As well as can be expected. He was disappointed, of course, that Robby wasn't at the farmhouse. But he brightened a little when I told him we've got Eve dead to rights and every reason to believe Robby's alive. He's feeling confident this time the exchange will go through, that these guys want the money," says Bradley. "I wouldn't be surprised if he's cracking open a bottle of bourbon as we speak."

The last bit makes Zack smile. "Tell him he can only have one, and you pour. This is far from over."

* * * *

Chuck Imperiale lives in an apartment building on a quaint, tree-lined street. Next-door is a cafe, and down the street, a restaurant and bar. Probably one he frequents. Upon arrival we're met by a middle-aged woman. She introduces herself as Torres' aunt, Judge Anita Lopez, and she has warrants for both Imperiale's place and Benson's. As always, Bradley delivers.

"Not too often a judge delivers a warrant herself," I say, shaking her hand.

Her smile is warm, but the eyes are steel. "Not too often I hear two cops are involved in a kidnapping conspiracy that local government and law enforcement officials might be tempted to cover up. I want this to go by the book."

Zack takes the warrants. "So do we. Right now Imperiale and Benson think they have a big payoff coming. They'll anticipate Maitlan will want proof of life before delivering the ransom. Right now, they're motivated to keep Robby alive. We don't want to do anything to complicate the equation for them. If they feel the heat, they might decide to run."

"And Maitlan's son would only be extra baggage. I get it. Bradley said as much when I asked him why a BOLO hadn't been put out." She purses her lips together and waits a beat before continuing. "Forgive me if I'm overstepping, Agent Armstrong. I understand this is your call."

Zack shoves his hands in his pockets. "Yes, ma'am. It is. But…"

The judge smiles. "This is my city. You've got a couple bad cops out there. But we have thousands of good ones."

"Trouble is, we don't know who the good ones are."

She nods, shakes our hands, then climbs into the car waiting at the curb.

"Best not fuck this up," O'Neill mutters.

Zack extends his arm in the direction of the steps that lead to an imposing security door. "After you."

O'Neill rings every bell and within a few seconds some well-meaning resident has let us in.

"That was easy," he says.

I pull out my Glock. "This next part might be a little harder."

Zack leads the way to apartment number two. He goes through the motion of knocking and announces us before deftly picking the lock.

It doesn't matter that we believe the apartment is empty; we go in, guns leading. After a quick sweep, our weapons are holstered.

"Looks like he uses the second bedroom as an office. I'll look through the desk, see if I can find anything," O'Neill offers.

"Robby hasn't been here," Zack announces with confidence.

We're alone in the living room. I take a moment to look around. Imperiale seems to live a simple but orderly life. The two-bedroom apartment is clean and uncluttered. "How can you be sure?"

He points to his nose.

Of course. Werewolf.

Zack disappears into the bedroom.

There's a stack of newspapers on the end table next to the couch. I leaf through them. "Looks like he reads the *Times* daily. But hasn't bought one since the day Robby was taken."

"He has an old desktop in here with the login and password pre-loaded. Doesn't look like he's logged into email since then either," O'Neill calls out.

Zack emerges, an evidence bag in one hand, a T-shirt of Imperiale's in the other.

I raise an eyebrow.

"Never can tell when it might come in handy." He slips the T-shirt into the bag and tosses it at me. "I'm going to ask O'Neill to wait here, keep the scene secure until forensics gets here to process it."

"Let me guess," I say. "We're heading to Benson's?"

"Yup. And we'll be leaving with his wife."

* * * *

Detective Benson lives with his wife in the Queens neighborhood of Sunnyside. Brick homes and small apartment buildings share quiet streets with tree-lined pathways. We pass a couple of big box stores and a slew of ethnic restaurants. Sprinkled between there are delis, bakeries, and trendy bars. It looks like an ideal neighborhood close to the city. As I step out of the car and look west, I can see the New York skyline.

"How long since you've been to the top of the Empire State building?" Zack asks.

I gaze at the iconic tower in the distance and flash back to a time when snow was falling and the winds were of gale force. Ethel and I had shut down the Onyx. Despite the lateness of the hour, we were able to gain access to the observation deck. It helps when your family owns the place. Ethel had just left her husband and we were living the good life, celebrating with cold champagne and Charlie Parker's red hot Jazz.

"Emma?"

I'm pulled back to the present. "Nineteen forty-nine. We're running out of time. They should be calling about the ransom drop in about an hour."

Zack is texting.

"Updating Torres?" I ask.

"Asking a favor of someone I trust. We need to keep this place secure until forensics can get here. The chances of Benson showing up to remove evidence are slim. But I'll feel better if someone's watching the house."

"How do you want to play this?"

"Mrs. Benson is eight months pregnant with their third. I don't want to upset her further."

"She's got one on the way, another she's about to lose." We walk in tandem up the sidewalk. "That's going to be impossible to avoid. Unless..."

"What are you thinking?"

Before I have a chance to answer, the front door opens. "Can I help you?"

Benson's wife is a pretty woman with red hair and rosy cheeks. She's dressed casually in an embroidered smock and leggings, her hands rest atop a very pregnant belly.

"Follow my lead," I whisper to Zack. Then I pull out my badge and approach with confidence. "Olivia Benson?"

"Yes," her response is hesitant.

"I'm special agent Emma Monroe. This is my partner, Zack Armstrong."

Olivia glances at my badge. "FBI?"

"Is Burt home?"

She shakes her head. "He's working a case. He couldn't come home last night. Are you working with him? Is something wrong?"

"May we come in?" I ask.

She steps back. "Of course."

"When did you and Burt last talk?" Zack asks.

"Yesterday afternoon. He called from a payphone to tell me he lost his cell phone and wouldn't be home until late tonight."

We follow Olivia to a parlor off the entryway. Polished wood floors and period furniture make the room both attractive and comfortable, a fire lends warmth. All together, it's a picture of domestic tranquility.

I take a seat next to Zack on the sofa. "Are your children home?"

Olivia's yet to sit down. Her anxiety is rising. "Madeline's at daycare. Joey's with my folks. I started having some contractions this morning. My doctor says I need to rest. Has something happened to Burt?"

"We believe he's safe," I assure her. "But he's mixed up in something dangerous. We think he's over his head. Things have gotten out of hand. We'd like you to take you into protective custody until we know for sure. He's going to be calling us, and we want you to help convince him to come in."

"What about the children?"

Zack answers, "Can your mother pick Madeline up from daycare?"

Tears start to well up in her eyes. "Probably. Yes. I'm sure she can. Is Burt going to be all right?"

"We hope so," Zack says. "Will you help us help Burt?"

"Of course." She wipes at the wetness on her cheeks. "Let me get my purse."

Zack rises. "We'd also like to a piece of clothing. Something he's recently worn. A T-shirt maybe."

She looks at us, a puzzled frown pulling at the corners of her mouth. "Why would you need that?"

"If we need to track him, it will help the dogs."

"Track him?" Alarm sends color into her cheeks. She clutches her belly.

I take her hand. "We don't expect to have to use it. It's just a precaution. I promise."

She doesn't look relieved, but does rise. "I'll get one from the hamper."

Once we're alone, I ask Zack, "Do you think she'll be able to convince Benson to turn himself in?"

He looks at me. "I do. But the real question is whether Benson will be able to convince Imperiale."

CHAPTER ELEVEN

It's a quarter to three when we pull into Maitlan's garage.

"Is this a safe house of some kind?" Olivia asks.

Zack is driving, I'm in the passenger seat. It's time to lay it on the line. "Have you heard anything on the news about the kidnapping of Roger Maitlan's son?"

"Of course, it was on the front page of the paper today and all of the stations are covering it." She stops abruptly, turns and looks back toward the entrance to the garage. "This is the building. The one Maitlan lives in."

"That's right," I say.

"Why would Burt be working a kidnapping case?" she asks.

Zack jumps in and answers. "We said we were worried Burt was mixed up with something dangerous. Olivia, he's been identified as an accomplice in the crime. He and his partner Chuck. They're demanding twenty million dollars ransom."

The color drains from her face. "That's impossible. Burt would never do that. Not ever."

"Not even for Joey? We've seen this before," I

say. "A good guy in a desperate situation is presented an opportunity and—"

She shakes her head vehemently. "No."

Zack unbuckles and gets out of the car. I do too. By the time I walk around to their side, he's opened the back door and is offering her a hand. "For your sake, I hope we're wrong. I really do."

She accepts Zack's assistance and clumsily climbs out. "The person who identified him?"

"Also an accomplice, " he replies. "She's in custody and hoping her cooperation will result in some kind of a deal."

"Will it?"

We head for the elevator. "I doubt it. She was the instigator. There's something important that I'd like you to remember, Olivia. According to our information, Burt was not the one who pulled the trigger that night. If we can get him to come in, to return Robby and testify against his co-conspirators, it could go a long way toward getting him a shorter sentence."

"Look, I don't know who did this, but I do know my husband. It's not Burt!"

We're inside the elevator now and it's climbing. In a couple minutes, Olivia is going to be in the conference room. A few minutes after that, she's going to hear her husband's voice, and her world is going to come crashing down.

"As you said earlier," Zack reminds her. "Your husband hasn't been himself for quite some time. He hasn't been sleeping. He's been anxious, depressed, stressed out of his mind. In a few minutes a call's going to be coming in, and we want you to listen in on it. Agent Monroe and I will be there, along with a couple other agents and Mr. Maitlan. We believe the call will be either from Chuck Imperiale or your husband."

The elevator door opens into the Penthouse. When we emerge, Roger is waiting for us.

His eyes dart from Olivia Benson's face, to her belly, and back again. His expression softens and he extends his hand. "Roger Maitlan."

"Olivia Benson." She winces. Her hands move to her stomach. "I'm afraid I need to sit down."

Roger and Zack exchange worried looks.

I place my hand on Olivia's back and wave her in the direction of the staircase. "There's a conference room downstairs. Maybe a cup of tea will help?"

She nods and moves in the direction of the stairs. "What is it, exactly, you want me to do?"

"When the call comes in, we just want you to listen. If you hear anything you recognize, we want you to tell us. If you identify the caller as your husband, we may want to put you on the line. At that point, you'll just need to talk from your heart. Ask him to give up his location, to let Robby go and turn himself in. Assure him we all understand what he's been going through. That he's not himself," I tell her.

Olivia's head is bobbing up and down.

When we enter the conference room, Bradley stands up. "Torres is pulling into the garage. She'll be here any minute." He extends his hand to Olivia. "Agent Bradley. We appreciate your help, Mrs. Benson."

I pull out a chair. "Why don't you take this one, Mrs. Benson?"

Zack moves to the console table that has the coffee and tea and begins to fill a cup with hot water. He holds up two tea bags. "Chamomile or Jasmine?"

"Chamomile, please."

"One minute to go." Bradley passes out headphones. "You'll be able to hear through these. Mr. Maitlan, pick up the handset on that landline when I tell you. Insist on speaking with Robby. As always, we'll coach you through."

"Did I miss it?" Torres enters just as the shrill sound of the phone's ring cuts through the air.

I make a quick introduction as I slide on a headset. "Agent Torres. Olivia Benson."

The cup of tea Zack made for Olivia hasn't been touched.

The phone rings again.

"Aren't you going to answer it?" she asks.

Maitlan places his hand on the receiver. His eyes are on Bradley.

"Go ahead. Pick up."

"Maitlan here." His voice is shaky. Whether from exhaustion or anxiety, I don't know.

Probably a bit of both.

The voice on the other side sounds almost as weary.

"Do you have the money?"

There's quite a bit of background noise—people having conversations, laughter—an undecipherable cacophony.

"Yes."

"Good. Now, here's what you're going to do. You know that little coffee shop down the street from you? When we hang up, you're going to head over there. There's a burner taped under the table in the corner, the one farthest from the door. Get it and wait at the table for my next call."

"I'm not doing anything until I speak to my son," Maitlan says.

I'm watching Olivia. She's listening intently, her eyes wide, her breath shallow. "It's not Burt, but you recognize the voice."

She turns toward me and whispers. "It's Chuck. I'm sure of it."

Maitlan continues, "I have your money. We're close. You're close. I want to talk to my son. I *need* to talk to my son. Give me that and we have a deal. I'll go get the phone. Follow your instructions to the letter."

Imperiale snorts. "You'll follow my instructions to the letter regardless."

Maitlan's standing now, pressing Imperiale as Bradley instructed. Being insistent but cooperative. "I need to know that my son is all right."

"You need to head over to the coffee shop. I'm hanging up now."

"No, I'm hanging up. Until I hear my son's voice, until I'm able to verify he's alive and safe, I'm not going anywhere." The receiver Maitlan's been speaking into comes crashing down so hard it pops back out of the cradle.

"Mrs. Benson identified the caller as Chuck Imperiale," I say.

Maitlan turns to Zack. "Did I just make a mistake?"

Zack gives his shoulder a squeeze. "He's going to call back." In three quick strides he walks over to the dry erase board in the front and picks up a marker. Let's play back the recording. See what we hear.

Bradley cues up the tape.

"There's a lot of noise in the background," says Torres.

O'Neill chimes in, "Music."

I close my eyes. Listen intently. "There's a bell," I add. "It sounds like an old-fashioned hotel bell. It's coming from different directions."

Zack's writing it all down. "There's more than one bell. I heard someone order a scotch rocks. That clunk, that's a glass being set down on a table or bar."

Olivia sits up suddenly. "I know where he is."

Bradley shuts off the tape.

The phone rings.

Zack holds up his hand. Looks at Maitlan. "Pick it up. Be cooperative. Tell your son you'll be seeing him shortly."

Maitlan reaches for the phone. "Robby?"

"Dad! I want to come home, Dad! I'm scared. I don't feel well."

The boy's speech sounds slurred. His response is slightly sluggish.

The billionaire pinches the bridge of his nose. "Listen to me, son. Everything's going to be all right. I'm going to be seeing you shortly. Be—" Maitlan's voice starts to crack. He takes a second to compose himself. "Be brave."

There's no response. The line is dead.

We all turn to Olivia. Maitlan is the first to speak. "Where are they?"

Olivia lifts the cup of tea to her lips and takes a sip, her hands are shaking. "When I first met Burt, I was fresh out of college and had moved back in with my parents. They live on the Island. We'd go to this dive motel off 112 called the Starlite. He mentioned it just the other day. Told me how a buddy of his busted a crack ring that had been dealing out of there. The Blue Moon bar is right across the parking lot. The bells. They have them on the tables so you can call your server over."

Zack starts giving orders. "Torres, go with Maitlan to get that phone and meet us in the garage. Bradley, get HRT on the line. Let's see how far out they are and if they can meet us at the location. O'Neill, I want you to follow in a separate car with Mrs. Benson."

"Me? It was Chuck, not Burt."

I place my hand over hers. "It's likely that Burt's with him. Until we know otherwise, that's our assumption. We'll want you to help us talk him out."

CHAPTER TWELVE

The Starlite is an old-fashioned motor lodge, two stories with doors opening directly onto the parking lot. I can imagine what the décor looks like. Worn chenille bedspreads, nightstands with a princess-style phone and one of those machines that will make the bed vibrate for a quarter, and a cathode ray TV hooked up to what used to be a state of the art VHS player.

Zack and I leave the rest of our team and Jastremski's agents from the HRT a quarter of a mile down the street. We pull into the Starlite's parking lot and select a space in front of the office. Dressed casually, we leave our vests in the SUV. I'm carrying a large tote bag. Zack is pulling a suitcase. The office smells like stale cigarettes and lemon Pledge. The knotted pine paneling covering the walls and reservations desk is gleaming. The linoleum floor, worn through in sections, is also clean and shiny. The Starlite may have seen better days, but someone has gone to lengths to keep the office spotless.

The woman behind the desk looks up when we enter. My guess is that she's in her late sixties. Her face is wrinkled, the skin thin like paper. Holding a

Danielle Steele novel in one hand and a cigarette in the other, she regards us with skepticism.

"Can I help you?"

Zack places his credentials on the desk alongside photos of Imperiale and Benson. "FBI. Where can we find these men?"

She shrugs, "I don't know, sweet cheeks, what makes you think they're here?"

Zack leans on the counter. "You give me their room number, we'll limit our search and rescue to that room. Otherwise we're going to have to sweep the entire building. The hotel will become a Federal crime scene. I heard the locals shut you down not too long ago. Bet that wasn't good for business."

She hands Zack a key. "They're in number one. The room on the far corner."

"How many other rooms are occupied?" I ask her.

She turns around, scans the board covered with keys. "Seven."

I follow her gaze. "Any of them adjacent to number one?"

She shakes her head. "No."

"Windows? Other exits?"

"Just the main door and the adjacent window," she says.

Zack turns around, lowers his head. "Torres?"

I hear her response in my earpiece. "Torres here."

"The suspects are in the room on the corner, number one. The front window and door are the only way in or out. Time to roll. As soon as the perimeter is secured, come in with Maitlan, Mrs. Benson, and O'Neill. You handle Mrs. Benson's call and keep Maitlan inside. O'Neill can oversee the evacuation of the other guests."

"Will do," Torres agrees

I hoist the tote bag over my shoulder. "Ready?"

Zack grabs the handle of the rolling bag and opens the door. "Let's go."

We head back toward the car, fire up the engine, and drive over toward room one. Just a couple tourists heading over to their room. I slip on my vest. A half-dozen other SUV's surround ours. HRT agents spill out of them, protective gear on, weapons in hand. Jastremsti quietly conveys orders. Two break off from the rest of the group and head upstairs to the second floor. Within seconds, they've quietly entered the room above number one.

I raise the bullhorn up to my mouth and press the lever. "Burt Benson, this is the FBI. You are surrounded. A call is about to come through on the line to your room. Answer it."

From my vantage point I can see Torres and Benson inside the office.

"Bradley?" Zack calls out.

"What can I do for you, boss?"

Some static comes through the line, then fades away.

"I want to hear the call."

"Figured as much. I'm ready," he replies.

"Dialing," says Torres.

The phone rings. It rings again.

I hold my breath.

When the third one is waning, Burt finally picks up.

"Hello?"

"Burt?"

"Olivia? Oh, God. You shouldn't be here. What are you doing?"

From my vantage point I can see inside the office, see Olivia start to crumble. Torres manages to get a chair under her before her legs give way. She's crying. "You shouldn't be here either Burt. They say you have the Maitlan boy, Burt. I told them..." She pauses, takes a deep breath, then continues, "I told them you'd never take a boy from his father."

Benson is crying too. "I'm sorry, baby. This isn't the way it was supposed to go. I'm doing this for Joey. Like Chuck said, it's the only way."

"Chuck's wrong. We'll find another way, a way that won't hurt anyone." Olivia's slowly rubbing her belly. She pauses again. Takes a few breaths. "I want you to listen to me, honey. I'm here with the FBI. Everything's going to be all right."

"It's not going to be all right. Everything's gone to shit, Olivia. I've fucked it all up."

"No. No, you haven't. You've been stressed and confused. We're going to get through this."

"Bradley, dispatch an ambulance. I'm worried about Mrs. Benson," I say.

"Ambulance on the way."

The line goes silent.

"Burt?"

"I'm here."

"I think the baby's coming, Burt. I need you with me. You're going to open the door slowly and sent that boy out. Then, when the Agents call for you, you and Chuck are going to come out of that room, hands in the air where they can see them. That's the way it's supposed to go right? That way no one gets shot."

"I can't do that, honey."

"Yes, you can," Mrs. Benson says through gritted teeth.

"I can come out," he says. "But—"

"But what?"

"Robby and Chuck aren't here."

The voice of one of the HRT Agents breaks through. "He's right. We have eyes in the room below. Benson's alone."

Torres grabs the phone. "This is Special Agent Torres. Where are they?"

"Chuck left with the kid about ten minutes ago. He was going to put Robby in the trunk and pick up a couple sandwiches at the Blue Moon. I'm coming out. I... I want to see Olivia."

The line goes dead.

The door opens.

Burt Benson comes out. Hands in the air. Eyes red-rimmed. Face tear-stained.

HRT moves in. Within seconds he's in cuffs. The hotel room swept.

"What kind of car is Imperiale driving?" I ask Benson.

He scans the lot, then tilts his head in the direction of the Blue Moon. "That black Chrysler over there the one next to the woods."

As soon as the words are out of Benson's mouth, the door to the office flies open and Maitlan runs out.

"Robby!"

Zack grabs my elbow. "If Imperiale saw us coming, he might have gone into the woods. If so, I can track him."

"Go," I tell him, then I take off after Maitlan.

He had a head start and he's an experienced runner. When I catch up with him he's banging on the trunk, prying at it with his bare hands and shouting out the name of his son.

Jastremski is right behind me with a crowbar. "Step aside."

The scrape of metal on metal sets my teeth on edge.

The trunk pops open.

A child is inside. Duct tape over his mouth and around his ankles. His hands are bound behind his back. His body is still, pale.

"Oh, no! No!" cries Maitlan.

Jastremski wraps his arms around the billionaire, pulling him back with the help of two other agents.

Maitlan is struggling to break free.

"I want my son! Let me have my son!"

I feel for Maitlan. But if the boy is dead, we can't disturb the scene.

Gingerly I reach inside and press my fingers to the side of his neck, searching for a pulse. The sights and sounds around me disappear.

Thump. Thump.

"He's alive. Get the paramedics over here."

I can hear the sirens getting closer.

Jastremski pulls a knife from a sheath attached to his utility belt and cuts through the tape around the boy's wrists and feet.

I rip the tape off the boy's mouth.

His eyes flutter open.

"Daddy? Is that you?"

Robby's speech is slurred, his eyes glassy. He tries to sit up, but can't quite manage.

"Robby!"

The agents holding Maitlan back let him go. He rushes forward, gathering Robby into his arms. They're both crying, but it's from relief.

The ambulance pulls up alongside us and comes to a stop.

I wave over the paramedics, then step aside and let them get to work.

Torres runs up. "Where's Zack?" she asks. Then she reaches for the arm of one of the paramedics. "There's a woman in the office over there, she may be in premature labor."

"We'll check on her as soon as the boy is stabilized," she assures Torres.

I step back, Torres follows.

The crew goes to work on Robby, transferring him to a gurney, checking his vitals.

"Where's Zack?" Torres asks again.

I turn toward the edge of the woods, then glance west where the sun is low in the sky. "He went after Imperiale. It'll be dark soon. Best get some flashlights and set up a grid search."

"Jastremski!" Torres calls out. "Any idea how far back the forest goes?"

Zack is the one that answers. His voice crackling over the radio. "About three-quarters of a mile. I've picked up a blood trail. It seems fresh."

"Blood trail?" asks Torres.

"And I have eyes on the suspect. He appears to be wounded. He's limping." There's a moment of silence then, "Charles Imperiale, FBI. You're under arrest."

CHAPTER THIRTEEN

"Damnedest thing." Bradley chuckles again.

"I tell you, I grew up on the island," O'Neill interrupts. "They're aren't any wolves. It had to have been a dog."

"Or a coyote," adds Zack, helpfully.

"Coyote?" Bradley asks, sounding skeptical.

Torres disappears inside of Maitlan's office. I assume for a little privacy. It sounds like she's on the phone, chatting with her kids.

The guys are packing up all of the equipment and I'm letting them. It's been a long few days.

Zack consults his phone. "Apparently, there are estimated to be more than twenty thousand in New York, more than five thousand in New Jersey."

"But on the island?" O'Neill asks.

Zack shrugs. "Yeah, even there. This website says the first official sighting of a coyote on Long Island was in early 2004 near Rockaway Inlet."

"Damnedest thing." Bradley repeats for the umpteenth time.

Torres emerges from Maitlan's office, bottle of bourbon in hand. "What do you say we toast before leaving? I doubt Maitlan will miss it."

"Hell, if he were here, he'd be pouring," Zack replies.

His phone rings.

"Armstrong. Speak of the devil. How's Robby?"

Zack steps out of the room. His voice drifts away as he moves down the hallway.

O'Neill passes some clean cups to Torres and she does the honors.

Bradley takes a sip then settles back in his chair, a look of contentment on his weathered face. "Now that's smooth."

"Got one for me?" Zack asks. He slides his cell phone back into his pocket.

Torres hands him his drink. "How's Robby?"

"Dehydrated. Still a little out of sorts. Looks like they were giving him liquid Benadryl to keep him docile. Fortunately, they didn't go too overboard. They're treating him with IV fluids and plan to monitor him through the night. Maitlan's going to stay with him."

We raise our cups and wish Robby a long life.

I check the time. "I should get online and find us a hotel. We're not going to get a flight out tonight."

"No need," says Zack. "Roger said we can stay here."

Torres finishes her drink and sets the cup down. "Well, I for one am heading home."

O'Neill picks up a box of equipment. "Let's get this stuff packed in the van."

Bradley takes it from him. "You have a shuttle to DC to catch. Zack and I can handle this." He looks at Zack. "Ri-guy here's got a date with his girl. Wouldn't want to stand in the way of true love now, would we?"

Zack hefts a box onto his shoulder. "No, sir."

There's a momentary pause with handshakes all around and a few slaps on the back for jobs well done. We're all tired and ready to move on, and yet there's a reluctance to separate. The case was intense, emotional. How could it be anything else with a child's life at stake? But we rose above it. We came together and we did our jobs. Robby is alive and safe. It's over. Time for Torres to return to her kids, for O'Neill to spend the evening with his girlfriend, and for Bradley to go home to... whatever Bradley goes home to.

Me? I want a long, hot bath and glass of cold chardonnay.

The others head down the elevator. I go to the kitchen, find the proper glass, then head for the fridge. There's a separate one for wine. The left side is stacked full of white, the right side full of red. The corkscrew is easy to find. In no time I have the bottle open, the perfectly chilled light gold liquid is creamy, buttery, with hints of vanilla and oak. Perfection. I take it with me into the bedroom and make my way through to the bath. With no case to solve, I can take all the time I need. I turn on the taps and dump in a handful of salts. By the time I've undressed and pinned up my hair, the large tub is a third full, the mirror steamed over. I step inside, lean back, and take another sip of wine. My mind drifts as the water rises, enveloping me in a warm cocoon.

I'm roused back to alertness by a knock on the door.

"Emma?"

I set my glass down on the edge of the ledge. Turn off the taps. "Yes?"

There's a long moment of silence. Then, "We did it, partner."

I ease my shoulders back under the water and smile. "We sure did."

I imagine him standing on the other side of the door, hands shoved in his pockets, eyes studying his shoes as he searches for his next words. "I couldn't have done it without you."

My response is instant. "Yes, you could have."

There's no reply. I wonder if he's left. If that's all he had to say.

"Zack?"

"Can I come in?"

There's not a hint of seduction in his tone. What I hear is impatience, frustration. Zack should be celebrating.

I sit up. "Is something wrong? Is it Robby?"

The knob turns, the door pops open. He fills the threshold, but he's careful not to cross it. "I don't want to do it without you," he says, his eyes connecting with mine. There's a lot of me to see, but his gaze is unwavering as he takes a sip of what looks to be a fresh bourbon on the rocks.

I pull my knees to my chest, wrap my arms around my legs. "Does that mean you won't be asking Jimmy for a transfer when we get back?"

He steps inside, closes the distance between us, then crouches down next to me. "Let me ask you a question."

I don't think I've ever seen Zack's expression so serious. "Okay."

"You've been all over the world. Yeah?"

"Yeah."

"If you could be anywhere, right now. Where would you want to be?"

I rest my cheek on my knee and study him before answering. "Here."

His hand snakes around the back of my neck. His lips hover over mine.

"Ditto," he says. Then he kisses me. His tongue takes my mouth, reclaiming it with confidence. The exploration is unhurried. Tender.

It leaves me aching for more.

"I won't be asking for a transfer," he whispers.

"Kiss like that, you must want something."

Zack pulls back and smiles wryly. "Well, I have to admit, the tub does look mighty inviting."

I slide forward. "And it's definitely big enough for two."

Zack douses the lights. "Hell, it's big enough for four."

There are no candles, just the glow from the lamp in his room. It casts us both in shadow. I close my eyes and remember back to another bath, another time, in Charleston. A time when I thought I'd never see Zack again. How wrong I was.

I hear the rustle of clothing being hastily removed, falling to the floor. Then he steps in and sits down behind me. Long legs skim my hips and thighs as they stretch out. Hands caress my shoulders and begin to knead at the knots that have managed to build up.

"How do we do this?" he asks me.

I settle back against his chest, his erection

presses into my back. "You seemed to know how to do it the other night in the alley."

One arm encircles my waist and pulls me closer. The other slides deep below the service of the water, fingers coax my legs apart then dip into my wetness.

"I should know what you like, what you want," he says. "But I don't. I don't know the things a lover should know."

I still Zack's hand, then pivot in the tub, draping my legs over his. "You know. You've always known."

He reaches for me, lifting me onto my knees.

I wrap my hand around his cock. It's long, thick, and poised at my entrance. I ease myself down.

Zack's eyes widen. His hips rise and fall beneath me as I ride him, slowly, deliberately. He latches onto my breast and sucks.

Together we move, bodies slick, breaths ragged. I can feel a tightness growing in my stomach. The pace is quickening. My knees are sore. My nipple raw. Every pull, every thrust is beautifully painful. I hold on tight and fly over the edge.

EPILOGUE

Day Four: Tuesday, September 8

I'm awakened by the smell of fresh brewed coffee and blueberry muffins.

I sit up in bed. "You're up early."

Zack hands me a cup of coffee. "It's after ten."

"Ten?"

He waves a plate in front of me. "Hungry?"

I set the coffee down on the nightstand and take the plate. "You went out and got muffins?"

"At the coffee shop down the street. Roger called. They're releasing Robby."

"I should shower and get dressed." I move to get up.

Zack walks over to the window and takes in the view. "No need to rush." He's wearing a pair of worn jeans and a dark grey sweater. The sun pouring in makes his hair looks lighter than it is.

I climb out of bed and go to him. "What now?"

He turns to face me. "Christ, you're beautiful." He smoothes down my hair, starts to lean in, then pulls back and answers. "I don't know."

I pull a throw off the end of the bed and wrap it around my shoulders to cover my nakedness. "Last night—"

"Was amazing," Zack finishes.

"But it wasn't enough."

"Honestly?"

My mouth is suddenly dry. My heart racing. I nod.

Zack shoves his hands inside his pockets. "I don't remember those other times. But somehow... Somehow I have the feeling we once had more. And, that in order to save this, we have to give up that. Am I right?"

Tears cloud my vision. My throat is tight. "Yes."

He pulls me into his arms. "Then that's what we'll do. For now."

I look up at him. "For now?"

He shrugs. "Sometimes things change."

Though not often in the pantheon. "Take the whole gluten-free thing, for example. I didn't see that coming."

"You never know what fate has in store for us, partner."

True. I've yet to earn my freedom, but at least I know the next case is one Zack and I will be working together.

Zack cocks his head and listens. "Elevator." His face lights up. "Robby's home. Clothes."

"Check. I'll be right out."

Robby. The boy we saved. The boy we brought home. One of hundreds, hell, thousands.

But he wasn't *the* one. That one is still out there, yet to be taken, endangered. Yet to be in need of saving. When they are, I'll be there. And, I'll be ready.

Why?

Because

Redemption could be one rescue away.

THE
BECOMING

ANNA STRONG VAMPIRE
CHRONICLES BOOK 1

JEANNE C. STEIN

FOREWORD

My name is Anna Strong. I was thirty on my last birthday, and I will be thirty when you read this. In fact, physically I will never be older than thirty no matter how many mortal years I have on this earth. I am Vampire. How I became, and what is the nature of my existence, is the reason for this story. I tell it the way it happened so you will learn the truth as I did.

It may not be what you expect.

CHAPTER ONE

It's one in the morning, late last July, and hot. I'm squirming around on the front seat of my car like a fidgety five-year-old. I can't even keep my fingers still. As if with a mind of their own, they drum a restless tattoo on the steering wheel.

David should have had Donaldson out of that bar thirty minutes ago. What can be keeping him?

I squint around the dark parking lot. I hate waiting. I'm no good at it. You'd think after two and a half years chasing scumbags—excuse me, alleged scumbags—for a living, I would have developed some patience.

I haven't.

I open the car door and step out. The dampness folds around me, a combination of heat, humidity, and a stubborn fog that clings to the Southern California coast like a soggy blanket. It's too late in the season for "June gloom." What happened to real summer, with a lazy sun and warm desert air to dry things out? Instead, the humidity plasters my silk blouse to my skin. Shit, it's like living in Florida . I shake out of a linen jacket and throw in onto the front seat before slamming the car door shut.

Impatiently, I smooth wrinkles out of my skirt. I should have taken the time to change into my usual work garb—jeans and a cotton tee. Besides being downright uncomfortable, these clothes remind me that I had once again subjected myself to a less-than-perfect dinner spent trying to justify my work to my parents. For the first time in thirty years I have a business of my own and real money in the bank. I'm happy doing exactly what I want to be doing. But is that enough for them?

Apparently not.

Of course, if they saw me now, standing in a smelly alley behind a storage building in a not-so-upscale San Diego suburb, they'd be convinced they are right.

Good thing they can't see me.

I draw in a breath, blow it out and look around.

What a place for a bar. The shabby clapboard building has only one light, a sputtering, feeble bulb against the wall. But there are at least fifty cars parked up and down the street and inside, raucous laughter and pulsating music, punctuated by the occasional wild cheer, reverberates like thunder on the still night air.

I draw another impatient breath. Two of the people inside that bar are my partner David, and our skip, John Donaldson. David and I are Bail Enforcement Agents, bounty hunters, and this shouldn't be taking so long.

Maybe Donaldson is giving David a hard time.

That thought brings a smile. My partner is 6'6", weighs two hundred and fifty pounds and was a tight end for the Raiders. He's big and looks mean, more than a match for John Donaldson, whose rap sheet showed a skinny, anxious man with thinning hair and wire rim glasses perched atop a bulbous nose—an accountant of all things.

I stretch and yawn, and do a few squats to stretch taut leg muscles, not easy when you're wearing three inch heels and a short skirt.

Still, there's not much chance he's giving David trouble. Besides the obvious, Donaldson is nothing but a white-collar wannabe who played fast and loose with his employer's retirement account. When they caught up with the idiot, his string of shady business deals had landed him in jail on embezzlement charges instead of in the morgue, where that same enraged employer threatened to send him. Fifty thousand dollars and some pricey La Jolla real estate got him released pending trial. He skipped about the same time his wife found out he'd been keeping a mistress. She became instantly cooperative. She wasn't about to lose her house because the creep decided to jump bail.

But the infidelity—that's her problem. We work for the irate bondsman who will be out a cool five-hundred-thou if we don't get him back in custody tonight.

Which is exactly what we intend to do.

This should be a piece of cake. Donaldson doesn't have a history of violence. Why he ran is still a mystery considering, as it turns out, he didn't run far. We discovered him holed up inChula Vista, in aSouthBay low-rent district, no less, with the same blonde bimbo who caused his wife to give him up. We assume he plans to beat it south to Mexico, but for whatever reason, he hasn't yet.

Still, he's been a slippery little bugger. We

thought we had him twice before and he managed to elude us.

But not tonight.

Tonight Donaldson decided to take a little excursion to a sports bar all by himself . It's a perfect set up. Once someone recognizes David, the reaction is predictable. And someone will recognize him—ex-football jock, local hero, David attracts attention the way the North Pole attracts a compass. Then it should be a simple matter of getting Donaldson's undivided attention. David will buy him a few drinks to loosen him up, maybe, or offer to show him his Heismann trophy or Super Bowl Rings. Anything to get him outside.

After that, it's a trip downtown, a little paperwork, and five thousand dollars deposited into our account in the morning.

Easy money. Especially for me.Tonight I'm the designated driver.

So what's the holdup?

I roll my shoulders. I want a nice, cool bath. I want out of these clothes. Come on, David, I repeat like a mantra, let's get this over with.

I can't stand waiting any more. The smell is getting to me. If I cross to the other side of the parking lot, I can look through the bar's front door and see what's going on. Maybe David needs a little help. A short skirt and high heels may be a better inducement to Donaldson than trophies and big diamond rings. And I'll still be close enough to beat it back to the car if they're on their way out.

Anything is better than cooling my heels in this stupid alley.

I start across. The throbbing bass is shaking the place and grows louder with each step. David must be deaf by now.

But it's not so loud that it drowns out a familiar voice bellowing across the lot. "Hey, Donaldson, where do you think you're going?"

Shit. Something went wrong. I reverse directions and scurry back to the car. I hear the thump of running feet before I actually see two shadowy forms sprinting toward me. No time for pepper spray or theTaser . And no way am I going to let this jerk get away from us a thirdtime . I unclip my .38 from my belt, take a deep breath, and wait for them to get just a little closer before I step out.

The gun has the desired effect.

Donaldson pulls up short, eyes riveted on the gun leveled at his middle. "What is this? What do you want?"

His face is devoid of color and looks different from his mug shot—leaner and meaner. His black eyes are sunk deep into their sockets and flash in the dim light like a cat's.

Those eyes are disconcerting, but I shake it off and put on a bright smile. "Let me give you a hint. You have a court date tomorrow. For some reason, your wife is afraid you might be planning to miss it. Might have something to do with that blonde you've been shacking up with."

David moves up behind him. He slips handcuffs from his pocket and leans his head close. "So, we're your escorts. No need to thank us.It's compliments of your full service bail bondsman."

Donaldson smiles, his mouth cracking in a cold,

humorless slit. "You work for Reese? Why didn't you sayso. Listen, I've got money. I can double what he's paying you right now." He steps toward me, his hand moving to a pocket in his jacket.

I take a step backward at the same time David grabs for his hand.

"Against the car," David barks. "Spread 'em."

But with amazing quickness, Donaldson ducks under David's restraining arm and is off again across the parking lot.

David groans. "I don't fucking believe this. Anna, start the car. I'll stop this bastard if I have to shoot his ass to do it."

I can't remember the last time anyone got away from David. Once he collars someone, they generally stay collared. This is definitely an annoyance. A sarcastic comment about David letting this guy get away springs to my lips, but when a gunshot explodes behind me, it dies in my throat.

For a moment, I'm frozen in place, hand on the car door. There is no longer the sound of running feet. David has disappeared. I crouch down, work my way around to the front of the car. Where is he? Did he actually fire at Donaldson? Did Donaldson have a gun? Shit, we hadn't gotten a chance to frisk the guy.

The taste of bile burns the back of my throat. Why isn't David calling out to me? I tighten my grip on the .38 and push to my feet. I know he must be hurt or he'd be yelling.

I'm trying so hard to see what's in front of me that when the attack comes, it's from behind and without warning.

Donaldson is suddenly beside me, wrenching my right arm back. The pain causes my hand to open reflexively and I watch my gun skid across the pavement. Then I'm slammed into the car.

"So, hot shot," he says. "What are you going to do now?"

His breath smells of alcohol and rage. He's knocked the wind out of me and I gasp for air. My right arm feels like it's going to snap. I fight to catch my breath, to keep the fear out of my voice. He's much too strong. "Get off me, Donaldson. You're breaking my arm."

He laughs, torquing my arm even higher. "Where's that partner of yours, huh? Maybe you'll be more cooperative now without him."

I try to straighten up, to take some of the pressure off my arm, but he pushes me back against the car with no effort. He's on something; he must be. I can't control the speed of my words, they tumble out in a rush. "Listen, Donaldson, you're already in trouble with the law. I know David must be hurt. Let me help him. We're not cops. You know you can leave now. Don't make it worse for yourself."

But he's still laughing, the sound so harsh and grating it seems to burn my cheek. "What makes you think I'm in a hurry to leave?"

I'm pinned against the car by his body. His hands begin groping. My stomach muscles constrict. I shove back against him, fighting to gain leverage. "Someone will have heard the shot in the bar. They'll come out."

But he cocks his head in the direction of the bar.

"With that racket? I don't think so. Go on, scream."

I do, yelling until my throat hurts. The noise from the bar swallows my cries.

"See? What did I tell you." He fumbles at the buttons on my blouse. "I think we should get to know each other better, don't you?" He gives up on the buttons and rips it open, spinning me around to face him.

I try to fight him off. I'm five-foot-five inches tall and weigh 125 pounds. He's not much taller or heavier, but he overpowers me as if I were a child. He grabs my hair and yanks my head back. He's got the door open, and he pushes me down onto the back seat. I gouge at his face and neck, drawing blood that looks thick and black in the dark. He acts like he's oblivious to the pain. I'm pinned under him, pitching and bucking against his weight, but I can't shake him off. He's unbuckled his pants, one hand holding me down, the other working at the zipper. I don't have room to kick at him, so in desperation, I reach between his legs and grab and squeeze.

In the darkness, I don't see the blow coming. There's a brief flash of exploding color. Then, nothing.

THE SACRIFICE

THE FORBIDDEN SERIES
BOOK 1

SAMANTHA SOMMERSBY

CHAPTER ONE

I felt myself flying backward. It happened in the blink of an eye. One second I was on top of the world, the next plunged into darkness, surrounded by the sounds of metal scraping against metal, shattering glass and terrified screams—one of them my own.

The railway car I was on had jumped the tracks. It was skidding sideways, momentum causing it to careen out of control. In the dim tunnel light I caught a glimpse of the rapidly approaching wall. The car crashing into it sounded like an explosion.

Then, just as suddenly as it had started, it ended. For a moment it seemed the earth stood still. Silent. I was wedged on the floor between two seats, my left arm and shoulder throbbing in pain. Using only my right arm, I reached for the seat in front of me and pulled myself up to a standing position. Without a moment's hesitation, I reached into my pocket for my lighter and struck a flame.

The air was thick with dust and debris that stung my eyes and filled my nose. I waved my hand in front of my face in an attempt to clear it. Squinting into the darkness, I called out for the woman who'd been in my arms just seconds earlier.

"Katherine?"

I spied her lying on the floor; she appeared unconscious. On impact she'd been thrown clear across the aisle. "Katherine!"

She didn't respond. I fell to my knees alongside her. Reaching out with a shaky hand, I offered up a silent prayer before checking for a pulse. Thankfully, she still had one and it was strong, steady.

I guided the light over Katherine's body, assessing her injuries. The butane burned and as seconds ticked away, the outer casing of the silver lighter became increasingly hot. Just as I noticed a tiny rivulet of blood seeping from her left ear, I dropped it.

"Bugger!"

The blood concerned me. The fact that she was unconscious concerned me even more. I pushed down the rising feeling of panic, then methodically began to search the area in front of me for the lighter. Within a few seconds I'd found it and was able to illuminate her face.

"Katherine, love, open your eyes."

Still no response.

"Henry? Where are you?"

It was the elderly woman Katherine and I had been sitting across from just minutes ago. It had been after midnight when we'd pulled out of the Mornington Crescent Tube station. There were only five of us in the car, Katherine and myself, the elderly woman and her husband and a young man.

I stood and held the light out behind me, in the

direction where the young man had been. I heard a cough and seconds later he emerged, stumbling down the aisle through the rubble and awkwardly stepping over a section of twisted metal frame.

"Is she okay?"

I remembered seeing the young man nursing a bottle in a paper bag as he boarded. He was obviously pissed, unsteady on his feet.

"I'm trying to find out. I need your help. Are you hurt?"

"No, I don't think so."

"I'm Wes. What's your name?"

"Mark."

"Mark, I need you to help me. I've been injured." I was suddenly acutely aware of the pain in my left shoulder. "I need for you to do as I say. Do you have a set of keys?"

"Yeah."

I handed him the lighter, then leaned over and opened one of Katherine's eyelids. "I'm a doctor," I explained. "Move the light up here, in front of her eyes."

With some relief I saw that Katherine's pupils were dilated, and although they were non-focal, they were still reactive to light.

I ran my hand over her hair. "Stay with me now. We'll get you out of here," I assured her before turning back to Mark.

"Remove her shoes. We need to check her motor response. That's it. Now, firmly run the key up the length of her foot."

For a second I held my breath.

"Like this?"

Katherine's foot retracted.

"Thank God!" I whispered. She'd clearly felt it.

"So she's okay?"

"Not by a long shot. But it could be worse. Much worse."

"What's wrong with her?"

"Head injury. She's had a bleed, I think. We've got to get her to a hospital."

"Somebody help me. Henry?" It was the elderly woman again and she sounded short of breath.

I leaned down, placed a gentle kiss on Katherine's forehead, then whispered, "Wait for me, love. I'll be right back."

My coat was crumpled under one of the nearby orange seats and I reached for it.

"Help me get this over her."

"What's wrong with your arm?"

"It's nothing." I climbed to my feet.

"Do you have a signal?" I asked, pulling my own mobile out of my pocket.

"No. You?"

"No. Let's check on the others."

Mark went first, holding the lighter out in front to show the way. First we reached Henry. He'd also been thrown across the carriage on impact, only his head had struck the window and shattered the glass. The scene was gruesome. The lighter went out, once again plunging us into darkness. I was almost grateful.

"Sorry," Mark apologized. He relit the flame, now holding the outside of the lighter with a bandanna he'd retrieved from his pocket. "The casing's hot."

Mark turned his head away from the dormant body. I couldn't blame him. The man's face was covered with blood; his neck had been partially severed by a section of glass. He was gone.

"Is he dead?"

"Dead?" The woman began to franticly call out for her husband. "Henry? Henry!"

I quickly crossed the aisle and crouched down next to her. "What's your name, love?"

"Margaret." She was struggling for breath. "Where's Henry?"

"Margaret, I'm a doctor. I'm going to try to help you. Are you hurt?"

"My arm. And my chest. It feels like something might have fallen on top of me. Where's Henry?" Her breaths were becoming more labored. "Henry!"

There was nothing on top of her chest. I checked her pulse. "I want you to calm down for me now. You're heart's beating like a humming bird. Do you have a heart condition? Do you take any medicines?"

"He's dead, isn't he?" Margaret looked me right in the eye. "Tell me!"

Before I could respond, the old woman gasped in pain and clutched her chest.

"What's going on?" Mark sounded panicked. "Is she dead, too?"

Things were going downhill fast. If we didn't act quickly, we were going to lose her. I bent over and placed my face next to Margaret's.

"She's not breathing and I've lost her pulse."

"Fuck!"

"Could be just a heart attack, but she was struggling for breath earlier. Could be an injury to the chest wall, or a collapsed lung, maybe an embolism. I'm a psychiatrist, for Christ's sake. It's been years since I've done this sort of thing and my left arm is useless! You're gonna have to help."

"Help do what?"

"Save her. Come over and sit by me. Give me your hand. I'll guide the chest compressions."

Mark dropped the lighter on the floor. "Damn it!"

"Leave it! Look, we don't have a lot of bloody time here. We need to open her airway. I want you to place your hand under her neck to tilt her head back and then pinch her nose, move her chin forward, and give her two breaths. Got it?"

There were a few scattered lights lining the left wall of the tunnel. My eyes had begun to adjust to the darkness and I could now see the outline of the woman.

"What if I do it wrong?"

"Do it!"

He did, then I leaned over the woman again to assess her breathing. Nothing. I reached for Mark's hand and placed it beneath mine on her chest.

"We're going to do chest compressions. Not too much force. Fifteen times. Ready? One, two, three, four," I counted. There was an audible crack. I felt Mark begin to pull back.

"I can't do this." He sounded as if he were about to cry.

"It's just a rib. Not so much force. Keep going all the way to fifteen. That's it. Now, breathe twice!"

We continued the cycle six times with no response.

"It's not working!"

He was right. For the first time in ages I felt incompetent. I'd been of no more use to Margaret than the pissed boy had been. I reached up and wiped the sweat from my brow.

"No, it's not working," I admitted, realizing that I had to accept defeat and move on. Katherine was still alive and she needed me, was depending on me.

"Now what?"

"Now we check on my girl. We've got to get her out of here."

I stood and made my way back to Katherine, Mark following closely behind.

"Maybe we should wait? Don't the Tube rails have electrical current flowing through them?"

"We'll be careful. I made a promise to the lady. I intend to keep it."

"Take a chance, Katherine. You know I'm right. You know it. You can feel it, can't you? You won't regret it, not for one bloody second," I'd promised her, leaning down to steal one more kiss, enticing her into wanting, into forgetting, into surrendering.

"We have no lights. What if they send through another car and they don't see us?" I asked him, before crouching down to examine Katherine again. "Ow! Bugger it!"

Pain shot through my arm and shoulder as my left elbow grazed a nearby seat. I rolled up my tie, placed it in my mouth, and bit down. Then I straightened my back, closed my eyes and tried to push the dislocated ball joint back into place. I couldn't manage it.

"Dammit!" I yelled, spitting the fabric out of my mouth, gritting my teeth against the pain.

"Christ, I could use a drink."

"Me too, Mark." I managed a small smile. "My shoulder's dislocated. You help me fix it and I'll buy you a bottle when we're out of here. Deal?"

"No. No way. What if it goes to pot? I didn't do so well with Margaret."

"You did fine. You'll do fine. This works ninety percent of the time like a charm."

"What do I need to do?"

"First you need to pull on my wrist with one hand and brace against my upper chest with the other. Pull gently, increasing the pressure until I tell you to stop. Then you'll hold that position, keeping the pressure steady for a bit."

"How long is a bit?" Positioning himself as instructed, Mark began to pull.

"Until it relaxes," I ground out.

"Relaxed yet?"

"Stop! Hold steady, now." I tried to breathe through the pain. My eyes were watering. "All right! Now, I need for you to rotate the joint back into place. Like this." I did my best to demonstrate. "Only at the same time."

"I don't know," Mark said hesitantly.

"Stop being a nancy! We're wasting time. Just bloody do it."

Mark closed his eyes, then took a deep breath. I took a breath too and steeled myself for what was coming. With a swiftness I was grateful for, Mark twisted the joints. The pain was excruciating, almost dizzying. I cried out in anguish as the bone clicked audibly back in place.

"All right?" asked Mark wrapping his arm around my waist. "You're not going to pass out on me, are you? I sure as fuck can't carry both of you out of here."

"No." I swallowed down the bile that had risen in my throat. "No, I'm not going to pass out."

The pain was subsiding. Gingerly, I tried to move my arm.

"Good job. It feels better. I have a bit more mobility."

"So I did okay?"

"You did great. I won't be able to carry Katherine out, though. I'm gonna have to ask you to do it. Can you do that, Mark?"

Before he could answer, the bright beam of a flashlight shined through the window of the carriage. Help was on the way.

CHAPTER TWO

I rode in the back of the ambulance with Katherine and one of the paramedics. As soon as we pulled into the bay I opened the rear door and jumped to the ground. Laura Stanton, trauma surgeon, burst through the double doors leading to Accident and Emergency. Eric Riley, the hospital's top neurosurgeon and a friend since medical school, was close in tow.

"Any change since the last radio report?" Laura asked.

"No." I was trying my damndest to not think the worst. "Laura, she's been out for nearly thirty minutes."

"What's her GCS?"

"Eight, I think. I'm not sure. It's been a long time since I've assessed—"

"Don't worry, you've done well. Let's get the patient intubated and into CT."

"Her name's Katherine."

"Katherine. Okay, then. You can come, Wes. But stay back and let us do our jobs. We're good at what we do. You know that. Right?"

She gave me an encouraging smile. I was glad

she was there. Laura was extremely competent. She had a quiet confidence about her, but not a shred of ego. More important than that? I trusted her.

"Right."

"Then let's get cracking."

I followed the trolley down the hall toward the trauma room. I made rounds at this hospital almost every day, but I'd never been in the trauma center, not once. I felt helpless, out of sorts. Six, maybe seven people crowded into the room. I stepped back and anxiously watched as the team of professionals quickly and efficiently went about their various tasks. Within minutes Katherine was stripped of her clothes and intubated, a ventilator breathing for her. Someone handed me a bag with her clothes in it. I set it on a nearby counter.

Eric ordered a CT with and without contrast, type and screen/cross. "I'll meet you in radiology," he said before walking out of the room.

Laura turned to the lab technician. "Did you get that?"

"Yeah."

"Run a CBC, Coag profile and lytes as well."

"Got it covered." The petite Asian woman began to search for a vein.

They were going to operate. I ducked out into the hall, my stomach in knots. "Eric!"

He paused and turned back to face me. "She important to you?"

I nodded.

"She'll be okay, Wes. Have I ever let you down?"

The question made me chuckle. "Too many

times to count." I looked him in the eye. "But never when it really mattered."

"Don't worry. I'll take good care of her."

The elevator arrived and Eric ran to catch it, leaving me alone in the long, sterile hall with blood on my hands and remorse in my heart. It was my cock-up, my fault that Katherine was in that carriage, my fault she was here. It was all my fault.

"Wes? I thought you might want to hold onto this." Laura placed Katherine's engagement ring in the palm of my hand. "We're taking her up to CT. We've got to get her registered. Is there family to notify?"

"Family? Yes. In the States. I'll take care of it." They wheeled her past me on a gurney. There were lines and tubes everywhere. It seemed surreal.

"Wes?" Laura was frowning. "Are you all right?"

"Me? Yeah. I'm fine. Go."

Laura started after the trolley. "Do me a favor. Go to A & E and get checked out, just to make sure?" she shouted back over her shoulder.

I agreed.

"Doctor?" The paramedic was standing just inside the entrance. He was holding Katherine's purse and my coat. "The belongings?"

"I'll take them." I reached into my pocket and pulled out my cigarettes. My hands were shaking, but I managed to get one out of the pack.

"Need a light?" he asked as we stepped outside into the cool night air.

"Thanks, I've got one." I sat on a nearby bench and began to search though my jacket pockets. Then

I remembered I no longer had my lighter. Mark had dropped it and I never picked it back up. I checked my watch. Had it really been just a few hours since I'd committed to abstain from the fags for the night?

"You smoke?" Katherine asked, surprise evident in her voice.

"Yeah." I placed the cig between my lips and flipped open the cover of my lighter.

"Didn't anyone ever tell you that's bad for you?"

"A man needs some vices." I shrugged.

"How come I didn't smell it on you earlier?"

"I showered? Hell, I don't know. Maybe you haven't gotten close enough." I stepped closer.

"Whoa there, cowboy! I agreed to a perfectly platonic dinner. Just two people eating food and watching a play." She pulled the cigarette out of my mouth and placed her hand on my chest.

"Together, like a date." Clearly I wasn't going to have time for a smoke.

"Date? This isn't a date!"

"It isn't?"

"No!"

"You sure?"

"Yes!" she said, getting increasingly flustered. "I told you, I'm engaged."

"I, for one, thought this was a date." I couldn't help but smile.

She changed the subject. "Why don't you quit smoking?"

"I guess I just haven't found the proper motivation. Tell you what, kiss me and I'll abstain,

from the fags that is, for the rest of the night."

"What about tomorrow, or the next day?"

"That depends," I told her as I leaned forward and lowered my lips to hers.

"On what?"

"On how well you kiss."

"What on earth are you doing here at this time of night? I thought you psychiatrists all kept normal business hours?"

Pulled back to the present, I noticed one of the critical care nurses coming toward me from the parking lot.

"Hey." I tossed the pack of cigarettes into the dustbin beside the bench.

"Jesus, what happened to you?"

I glanced down at my shirt. It was spattered with blood. When I looked back up, the nurse was staring at Katherine's bag. I'd almost forgotten it was there.

I picked it up and started to search through the contents. There was a gold compact, a tube of lipstick, a wallet and a mobile phone. I pulled the phone from the bag, opened it up, glanced at the display, then snapped it closed.

"Dr. Atherton?"

"Hm?"

She had taken a seat next to me, concern etched on her face. "What happened?"

My eyes burned. My head was pounding. I didn't know where to start.

"There was an accident, in the Tube," I finally managed to choke out. "My date, Katherine, she uh…she…"

"She got hurt?"

I nodded. "It looks like she has a subdural. She's in CT now. I think Eric's going to do a crainy. I've got to call her mum."

"Can I help?"

"No. Thanks. I can handle it. I'll see you up on the ward in a bit. Katherine will be coming your way, no doubt."

The nurse nodded. "She's in good hands with Mr. Riley."

"I know. Go on. You're going to be late for your shift."

"I'll have a fresh pot of coffee waiting," she promised before walking away.

I took a deep, steadying breath, opened the mobile once again and started to scroll through the recently dialed numbers. George. Damien. Mom work. Home. I dialed home.

"Hello?"

"Hello, Mrs. Lawson? My name is Wesley Atherton. I'm calling from London. I'm a friend of Katherine's—"

"Has something happened to Kate?"

I took a fortifying breath and then tried to calmly explain.

"I was out with your daughter tonight. We had dinner and went to the theater. We took the Tube and on the way back... Well, there was an accident. The carriage we were in derailed. I'm afraid Katherine was injured."

"Can I talk to her?"

"She's being evaluated. They're doing a CT now. She's unconscious. She may need surgery."

"What kind of surgery?"

"Neurosurgery."

"Dear God," Katherine's mother gasped.

"We'll know more shortly. I'll call you back when there's news. I'll have her mobile if you want to reach me."

"Let me get a pen. What was your name again?"

"Wesley Atherton. Dr. Wesley Atherton. She's in good hands, I assure you."

"You're a medical doctor?"

"I'm a psychiatrist."

"Where is she? What hospital?"

"We're at Saint Catherine's, in Camden Town."

I walked back into the hospital and headed for the radiology department.

"Dr. Atherton?"

"Wes," I said. "Call me Wes. And you are?"

"Julia. Don't lie to me, Wes. It's bad, isn't it?"

"It could be. The truth is, we don't have enough information yet."

"I'll be on the next flight. If Kate wakes up, tell her I'm on my way."

"Will do."

I pushed through the swinging double doors. The receptionist behind the counter pointed me to room three.

"I'm counting on you to take care of her," Julia said.

"You have my word," I assured her before ringing off. "What's the verdict?" Eric and Laura were standing in front of a series of images.

"See this?" Eric pointed to the film. "The hyperdense crescentic mass—"

"Subdural hematoma?"

"Exactly. I'll make a couple burr holes, to relieve the pressure. I say we continue conservatively for now, a corticosteroid, to reduce the inflammation and swelling, and an anticonvulsant to control her seizures."

"She had a seizure?"

"A mild one. It didn't last long. Let's scrub," Eric said. "The sooner we get her in, the better."

"You haven't had your shoulder looked at yet, have you?" Laura asked as she backed out the door.

"I'm heading over to the A & E now. Anything happens..."

"I'll page you," she assured me.

* * * *

"Jesus, Wes, I heard what happened. Sorry to keep you waiting. It's been a crazy night," said the resident.

"No worries. I've already had the x-ray."

"I saw it. Did you really get some kid to pop your shoulder back in?"

"Where did you hear that?"

"The paramedics that brought you in. Is it true?"

"Yeah. How's the x-ray look?"

"Kid did a great job. You'll need to keep it immobilized for a week or so. You should see an orthopedist though."

He wrote out a prescription, then handed me the slip of paper. As soon as I read it, I tried to give it back.

"I don't need that. Just give me a couple ibuprofen."

"You say that now. Fill the prescription that way if you need it, you'll have it."

As he left the examination room I heard him call out to one of the nurses. "Some ibuprofen and a sling for Dr. Atherton here. We need to immobilize his shoulder."

I leaned back against the wall. The evening had started off so well. I closed my eyes and a series of images washed over me.

The wind blowing Katherine's hair in her face as we walked to the restaurant. The sideways glance she threw my direction during dinner when she thought I wasn't looking. I lifted the collar of my shirt and inhaled. I could still smell traces of her on it, where she'd comfortably rested her head during much of the play.

I remembered the way she'd laughed as we ran from the theater to a taxi in the pouring rain. How her breath hitched when I'd pulled her close in the back of the cab. How she'd gasped, opening her luscious mouth to invite me in when I crushed my lips to hers.

Even now, I could almost feel the curve of her breast beneath my hand. The way her nipple had hardened through her bra and silk blouse when I'd brushed my thumb across it. The warmth of her breath. Those deliciously intoxicating panting sounds she'd made as I kissed down the long column of her neck and across her collarbone. Her lustful moan as I slipped my hand up her leg, under her skirt. And the exquisite realization that her legs were willingly parting for me, in encouragement, in need.

> *"Wes," she moaned. "Don't. Stop."*
> *"I won't," I assured her. "I'll never stop."*
> *"No. I mean, stop. He's...he's watching us,"* Katherine whispered. *"What am I doing? This isn't me."* She was gasping for air, her chest rising and falling rapidly in the heat of passion.
> *"Let him,"* I growled, crushing my mouth to hers in another demanding kiss as my hand continued the forbidden journey under her skirt and up her leg.

I was getting hard again, just from the mere thought of her.

"So, do you need some help with that?"

My eyes flew open. I hadn't heard the nurse come in.

"The ibuprofen." She nodded toward the sealed packet and cup of water on the bedside table.

"No, thanks. I've got it." I picked the packet up with my good hand, tore it open with my teeth, and poured the two tabs out onto my waiting tongue. I dropped the empty packet back onto the tray, then washed the pills down with a swig of water.

"Dr. Atherton to recovery. Wesley Atherton to recovery," came the overhead page.

"I've got to go."

"Let's get this sling on first."

She worked quickly, then sent me on my way. The elevator took too long, so I opted for the stairs.

Eric was waiting for me in the hallway outside

of recovery to escort me to Katherine's bedside.

"She came through the surgery just fine," he said as we walked. "Her vitals are stable. We'll keep her here for a while longer, just to make sure, then she'll go up to ICU."

"Okay."

The recovery room was cold. Katherine looked small and pale against the stark white sheets.

"Sprain?" He nodded toward my sling.

"Dislocated shoulder. I'll be fine."

Eric looked like he had something to say. Normally he wasn't one to hold back.

"Out with it."

"Laura seems to think that the two of you are engaged."

I slid my free hand into the pocket of my trousers and fingered Katherine's ring.

"Well, she's half right," I admitted, remembering the moment we first met.

"Here, take my seat." I offered my seat to the elderly woman who'd boarded at Moorgate Station.

"That was nice of you."

I shrugged off the compliment. "Yeah? Well, don't tell anyone. I've got a reputation to uphold."

I turned around and looked into the most beautiful pair of green eyes I'd ever seen.

"What? I have spinach in my teeth, don't I? I knew I should have chosen the pasta salad for lunch."

I grabbed hold of the bar she'd been holding on to so that my hand was positioned adjacent to hers. "No. It's your eyes. They're stunning."

"Are you sure there's no spinach?" she asked, grinning widely, showing me her teeth.

"No spinach," I confirmed. "You're American?"

"Yup! Guilty as charged."

"Visiting?"

"Here for a few months, finishing my masters."

As we pulled into the next stop I glanced down and noticed the ring. The car lurched, throwing the American off balance and she bumped into me. Without thought I reached out and wrapped my arm around her waist. As soon as I was able to steady myself I apologized and let go.

"Sorry."

"It's okay." She looked away shyly.

"Really?" I slipped my arm back around her waist. "Have dinner with me."

"What? No! What are you doing?" She pushed my arm away.

"You said it was okay."

"Because it was an accident. I'm engaged." She held up her hand and wiggled the finger that held her engagement ring.

"That is not an engagement ring."

"What do you mean?" She pulled her hand back and looked at the classically simple solitaire. "Of course it's an engagement ring."

"You're not going to marry him. He's all wrong for you."

"You don't even know him. You don't even know me. I take it back. You're not nice after all." She turned around.

I leaned down and whispered in her ear, "So have dinner with me. Convince me that the two of you are perfect for one another and I'll apologize."

She turned her head slightly. "No."

"Please? Look, I'd rather not beg, but I'm not above it. Agree or I'm going to have to fall onto my knees in supplication. It's likely to be embarrassing for you and a bit humiliating for me but what the hell? You're worth it." I hitched up one leg of my trousers, preparing to kneel down.

"You don't have to do that." She reached for my elbow, preventing me from fully kneeling in front of her.

"Fantastic! So, how does Italian sound?"

"I'm not having dinner with you."

"You agreed," I pointed out. Looking around, I asked our fellow passengers, "Didn't she consent?"

Four or five of them nodded.

"See?"

"Do you always get your way?"

I shrugged. "Pretty much."

"Well, not tonight," she declared as we pulled into her stop. "Mr. — "

"The name's Wes."

She moved to walk away. I reached out, just barely grazing the back of her hand with my fingertips. "And you are?"

"Katherine." She turned to go, not looking back. Not until she got off, that is. Just as we pulled out she spun around. For the briefest of moments our eyes locked, then she was gone.

"Christ, you know how to pick them," Eric said. "First Reese, now you're dating a woman that's engaged to someone else?"

"Katherine wouldn't say we're dating."

"You were out together."

"We had dinner and went to the theater."

"And you were heading back to your place?"

"You make it sound sordid. It wasn't like that. It isn't like that. It's complicated."

"I can imagine having a girlfriend with a fiancé can get pretty complicated."

I ignored his jibe and pressed on. "After that first day we kept bumping into one another on the Tube. She'd board at the same stop, like clockwork. We'd chitchat, that's all."

"Until?"

"The fourth day. It was raining outside and Katherine had forgotten her umbrella. She was drenched when she boarded. I tried to get her to take my mine so she wouldn't catch her death, but the silly bint wouldn't listen. I almost let her get away with it too. But just before the door closed, I ran out."

"You walked her home."

"We stopped for a cuppa just down the street from the flat where she's staying. We were in the café for hours. Just as we were about leave, I got an emergency call, an admission. I left her with my brolly."

"In exchange for her number?"

I shook my head. "No. Didn't even ask as a matter of fact."

"Wesley, wait!"

It was pouring rain. I'd walked only a few meters and already I was soaked. I turned back.

Katherine was standing under the awning of the shop, umbrella open. She was holding it out to me.

"You forgot your umbrella!"

"You can give it back to me tomorrow."

"What if I don't see you tomorrow?"

The thought hadn't occurred to me. I returned to the shelter of the awning, pulled out a business card and handed it to her.

"Call me," I said, then I dashed off.

"And she called you?" asked Eric.

"Later that night, to thank me. Seemed like we talked forever, about everything and nothing. We really connected. You know?"

"Wes, you're a shrink. You're a professional listener. You connect with everyone."

"Not like this. As we were about to hang up I noticed a pair of theater tickets sitting on my desk. I've yet to cancel my father's box. I keep meaning to, just haven't gotten 'round to it."

"So you asked and she accepted."

"Yeah. I'm telling you, Eric, the second I laid eyes on her I—"

"Does he know?"

"Does who know what?"

"Her fiancé. Has anyone called him about the accident?"

"Bollocks!"

"I take that as a no?"

"I called her mum. Maybe she called Damien?"

"That's the fiancé?"

"Yeah." I checked my watch. "It's been a while since we spoke. Surely she's called him by now."

"One way to find out," Eric replied. "Can I get you anything? I'm going to grab some coffee."

"No thanks." I pulled out Katherine's mobile and rang Julia. There was no answer. Not at home and not on her mobile. So, I tried Damien.

He picked up on the third ring. "Hello?"

"Hello, is this Damien?"

"Who's calling?"

"This is Dr. Wesley Atherton. I'm calling from Saint Catherine's Hospital, in London. I need to speak with Damien, it's about his fiancée."

"This is Damien. What's wrong with Katherine? Is she sick?" He sounded appropriately concerned. He was probably a nice guy. I didn't want him to be a nice guy.

"Who's Katherine?" It was a woman's voice.

"Shh," Damien hissed. Muffled words were exchanged.

"Are you still there?" A bell was ringing in the background.

"Yes. Yes, I'm here."

"Do you need to get that?"

"No. Go on."

"There was a derailment late last night, near Camden Town. Katherine was on it and she sustained a head injury."

"But she's okay?"

The voices in the background were getting louder.

"She needed surgery. She's stable now but—"

"Julia!"

"How dare you!" a woman shouted.

I pulled the phone slightly away from my ear.

"It's not what it looks like."

"Don't insult me, Damien. It's exactly what it looks like! Christ, the girl answered the door wearing a sheet. Do you think I'm an idiot? Kate's in the hospital and you're—"

"We aren't having this discussion now. Kate's condition, it's serious, Julia," he said. "I have her doctor on the phone."

"Give me that! Hello? This is Julia Lawson, Katherine's mother."

"Julia, it's Wes. I tried calling you a few minutes ago to see if you'd spoken to Damien. When you didn't answer I thought that maybe I'd better ring him."

"I left my purse in the car when I ran up here. How's Kate?"

"She made it through surgery just fine. She's stable. They'll be moving her up to intensive care soon."

"Is she awake? Can I talk to her?"

"I'm afraid she's still unconscious. But that's nothing to be alarmed about at this point. Are you on your way to the airport?"

"Yes. I'll see you soon."

"I'm coming with you," Damien interjected. "It'll just take me a few minutes to shower and pack."

"Don't bother," I heard Julia say.

"You can't stop me. You know she'd want me there."

"She would want the man she thought you were there. But you're not him. You're not even close." Then the line went dead.

S. J. Harper is the pen name for the writing team of **Samantha Sommersby** and **Jeanne C. Stein**, two friends who met at Comic- Con in San Diego and quickly bonded over a mutual love of good wine, edgy urban fantasy, and everything Joss Whedon.

Samantha Sommersby left what she used to call her "real- life" day job in the psychiatric !eld to pursue writing full-time in 2007. She is the author of more than a dozen novels and novellas including the critically acclaimed *Forbidden* series. She currently lives with her husband and terrier pup, Olive, in a century-old Southern California Craftsman. Sam happily spends her days immersed in a world where vampires, werewolves, and demons are real, myths and legends are revered, magic is possible, and love still conquers all.

Jeanne Stein is the national bestselling author of *The Anna Strong Vampire Chronicles*. She also has numerous short story credits, including most recently the novella *Blood Debt* from the *New York Times* bestselling anthology *Hexed*. Her series has been picked up in three foreign countries and her short stories published in collections here in the U.S. and the U.K. She lives in Denver, Colorado, where she finds gardening a challenge more daunting than navigating the world of mythical creatures.

For more information on other books by **S. J. Harper**, please visit their official website: SJHarper.me

Also by S. J. Harper